GREEN PEACHES RIPEN

GREEN PEACHES RIPEN

*

MARY MULLER

THE
COMPANION BOOK CLUB
LONDON AND SYDNEY

This edition, published in 1982 by
The Hamlyn Publishing Group Ltd,
is issued by arrangement with
Souvenir Press Ltd.

THE COMPANION BOOK CLUB

The Club is not a library; all books are the property
of members. There is no entrance fee or any pay-
ment beyond the low Club price of each book.
Details of membership will gladly be sent on
request.

Write to:
The Companion Book Club,
Odhams Books, Rushden, Northants.

Or, in Australia, write to:
The Companion Book Club,
C/O Rigby House Books, P.O. Box 252
Dee Why, N.S.W. 2099

*Made and printed in Great Britain
for the Companion Book Club
at The Pitman Press, Bath*
600 872868
1182/385

To Joy Packer

AUTHOR'S NOTE

All the characters in *Green Peaches Ripen* are entirely fictitious.

MARY MULLER

Constantia,
Cape Peninsula

Chapter One

WE LIVED IN a small flat in the centre of Pretoria. My mother and I were alone because my father died when I was three.

She earned our living by making clothes for a small select group of wealthy women. When I returned from school and opened the front door I'd often hear the soft whirr of her sewing machine. Sometimes I found her at the table cutting out, the floor around her strewn with bright snippets of rich material. At other times she'd be sitting quietly sewing by hand, and would look up and smile as I came in. She was always there, and always the same.

We lived frugally but there was enough to eat, and our meals were prepared with the same care and imagination as the clothes she designed for her wealthy customers.

Each year I accompanied her to the spring and autumn sales. It was an education to shop with her. She fondled the silks, velvets and other materials with her slim white fingers, caressing and rubbing them softly against her cheek, putting them to her lips and sometimes even smelling them. With the eagerness of a hunting-dog she'd pounce on a remnant of silk, and its texture, subtle shading and opulence lay revealed to me.

She gave me love, security and companionship.

How many times I must have asked her to repeat the story of her marriage to my father. 'Mom. Tell me the story of you and Dad.'

She'd look at me and smile, touching the shining neatly coiled hair in the nape of her neck. 'You've heard it so many times Anna.'

'Tell me again. Please, Mom!'

She'd settle herself comfortably in the chair, her head bent over her sewing. 'As you know, I was born in England and lived with my parents in London. My mother was a very pretty woman – and a very spoilt one! She was the only child of doting wealthy parents, who pandered to her every whim; when she married my father he too was unable to deny her anything. Your Uncle Charles and I were tractable children, so she had no difficulty in dominating and ruling her household.

'When I was eighteen she sent me to a finishing school in France. She was ambitious that I should make a good marriage. It was at this school that I met your god-mother, Trina Marais. She came from the Cape and we immediately became friends. My mother didn't like her. She referred to her as "that vulgar little colonial", and did all she could to discourage our friendship. But I loved Trina – she was warm, kind and strong. I was painfully shy and though she was small she always protected and helped me. When I returned to England I was launched into society. My mother gave a Ball and worked indefatigably on my behalf, but I was hopelessly shy and my social début passed unnoticed.' She smiled whimsically.

'Go on Mom! Go on!'

'Trina went back to the Cape and shortly after married Jan de Villiers and went to live at Wonderkloof, the family farm. The following year Johan was born, and she asked me to be his godmother. Four years slipped by

10

and I seemed destined to become an old maid. Then one day, the housemaid knocked on my door and said there was a gentleman to see me in the drawing-room.'

At this part of the story I always wriggled with excitement. 'Yes. Go on Mom, go on!'

'He was standing at the window looking out on the Thames, and turned to face me as I came in. He was tall and dark, and his right eyebrow tilted humorously. "I'm Paul van Reenen," he said. "Trina asked me to look you up when I came to London."' She smiled. 'That was the beginning Anna. I saw him nearly every day.' At this stage her face would become strained. 'My mother didn't like him. She called him "that common young man" or "that oafish colonial". When he returned to South Africa we wrote to each other every week – then suddenly he stopped writing and for months I heard nothing.'

'You loved him, didn't you Mom?'

'Yes. It was Trina who brought us together. One day she met Paul and asked him if we were still corresponding. He told her that I hadn't answered his last two letters. Trina's eyes flashed and she said "Lorraine never got your letters, Paul. That wicked old witch read and tore them up. I'm certain of it!" She says his face lit up and he grasped her hands and said "D'you think so Trina?" – "I don't only think so," she said. "I'm certain of it!" Paul had very little money, but he took the next boat to England. I was in the garden when he walked up our drive. He saw me and crossed the lawn – this time he didn't smile. He looked stern and said, "Lorraine, did you get my letter?" – "What letter?" I asked – and he took my hand and said "I wrote and asked you if you would marry me."'

'Go on Mom, go on! What did you do?'

She always smiled and a faint touch of colour would warm her pale cheeks. 'I threw myself into his arms!'

I'd expel my breath in a rapturous sigh.

'I wanted to elope, but Paul would not hear of it. That evening he came to see my parents. My mother was cold and rude – she treated him like a lackey. When Paul asked my father if he could see him alone, she said in a clear scornful voice, "There's nothing you could possibly have to say to my husband that I shouldn't hear." So he gave a courtly old-fashioned bow and said he wanted to marry me. Oh Anna, she said such cruel and terrible things and finally accused him of being a fortune hunter. He turned to me and said, "D'you believe that Lorraine?" I shook my head and he took my hand and said, "Will you come away with me now – tonight?" and I said "Yes. I'll go upstairs and pack my bag" – but he stopped me. "No," he said. "You'll take nothing with you. Take off those pearls you're wearing, and your rings and diamond brooch. Tomorrow I'll buy you clothes, and you'll send that dress you're wearing back to your mother." She suddenly screamed hysterically and flung herself back on the sofa, drumming her heels like a small child. My father ran and put his arms around her, then turned to me and said "Go! For the love of God, go!"' She smiled humourlessly. 'And that's the last time I saw them.'

'Did you hate them Mom?'

'Not then. I wrote to them when you were born and didn't really expect a reply. I wrote again when your father died. There was no reply. Yes, after that – I hated them.'

My mother often spoke about her brother Charles. 'He always tried to help me. After our parents died he wanted me to inherit equally but I wouldn't accept a penny. I knew Paul wouldn't like it. Charles has been a good godfather to you. Every year he puts a hundred pounds in trust. At twenty-five you'll have a nice little nest egg. When I've saved enough we'll visit them in Surrey. He's a kind man – you'll like him.'

Our happiest times were the holidays we spent each Christmas with my godmother on her farm Wonderkloof at the Cape. My mother always had something wrapped in tissue paper for Trina. A rich silk blouse; a vivid linen suit or a flamboyant cotton dress – always in brilliant colours because my godmother, small elegant and sunburnt, was like a brightly plumaged bird. She was a widow and her name was Katrina Johanna de Villiers – but everyone called her Trina.

When we returned to Pretoria and I lay in bed listening to the hum of traffic in the streets below, I'd remember the silent nights at Wonderkloof – the only sound the creaking of a floorboard, the distant bark of a dog at the coloured cottages, the chirping of a cricket or the haunting eerie hoot of an owl.

At school I sat at my desk and dreamed. Bright cameos were etched in my memory – the white square homestead gleaming brilliantly in the sun; the oak front door exquisitely carved with leaves and acorns; the cool T-shaped hall looking on to the vine-trellised courtyard, filled with Trina's ferns and potted plants; the gnarled pomegranate which shadowed the walls of the thatched-roofed dairy – its hard red fruit split open, revealing the transparent magenta pips; and the curved marble seat and sculptured cypresses at the end of the long swimming-pool.

I could see Trina walking in her garden, dwarfed by her wide-brimmed straw hat, carrying her boat-shaped basket in the crook of her arm.

I'd remember Johan on Christmas Day, dressed up as Father Christmas and speaking in a strange deep voice. The *volk*, (coloured labourers and their families) dressed in their best, standing at the foot of the wide

13

steps in the shade of the old oaks. The numerous broods of children for once spotlessly clean with their noses wiped. As Trina called their names each child, smiling shyly, climbed the steps to receive a present and a pat on the head from Father Christmas. Sometimes a small child screamed when its name was called, clinging to its mother and desperately burying its brown face in the folds of her skirt. I always thought Johan overplayed his part. His booming voice was enough to make any one of them quail and pale with fright.

But the brightest memory of all was the first time I saw the *kloof* after which the farm is named.

One morning we were having breakfast when Trina looked across the table and said, 'Johannes, when are you going to show Anna the *Kloof*?'

She was the only person I knew who called Johan by his full name. At nineteen he was a provincial rugby player and would soon become an international one.

I was a lanky fourteen.

'You don't have to take me,' I said quickly. His grey eyes smiled at me, 'I wouldn't miss showing you the *Kloof* for anything!' He turned to Trina. 'Ma, you organize food and I'll take Anna there on Sunday. I'll ask Julian and his girlfriend to come with us.' He fiddled with his fork. 'I'll also 'phone Lynette.'

'Is that Lynette van Tonder?' Trina asked a shade sharply.

'Yes Ma.'

'A pretty girl,' she turned to my mother. 'But the poor child has an unfortunate nasal twang inherited from her mother.' She dropped her voice confidentially. 'I once shared a room with her at school. D'you know my dear, that voice nearly drove me mad. Fortunately I was able to move to another room without hurting her feelings.'

14

'I want to go too!' Pieter shouted, spluttering porridge over the table.

'No Pieter,' she said firmly, 'it will be too much for you.'

He scowled. 'I think it's damn unfair!' he muttered.

'Pieter,' she stared at her eight year old son sternly. 'There'll be no swearing in this house.' She was always saying that, as though Wonderkloof was a special holy place.

Johan was frowning and took longer than usual to finish his breakfast. Pieter and I sat and watched him. When he'd finished he looked up and saw us staring at him, and grinned. 'Are you two coming?'

We leapt to our feet and followed him out of the room to tag at his heels until he joined the *volk* on the lands. This was our daily routine.

On Sunday we left for the *Kloof* in the early morning while it was cool. It was midsummer and the sun blazed in a clear blue sky – as we steadily climbed the mountain slopes the heat became oppressive, the sweat poured down my face and I started to flag.

Johan was striding easily ahead and stopped, waiting for me to catch up. 'Are you very tired?' he asked taking my arm and smiling at me kindly. I shook my head panting, and wiped my forehead. 'Look,' he pointed. 'Now we have the first good view of the *Kloof*.'

Thickly wooded with evergreen indigenous trees it made a deep green indentation in the smooth velvety flanks of the mountain. As I continued wearily climbing the steep slope the trees separated and revealed a slender silvery waterfall cascading over the edge of a high cliff in a misty plume of fine spray.

'We'll picnic on the upper ledge,' Johan said. 'There's a grove of trees and a stream. If you look back you'll see a magnificent panoramic view of the farm.'

I stopped and looked. I could see the square outline of the farm-house nestling amongst the oaks which hid the gabled cellar; the silvery-grey poplar wood at the end of the paddock; the softly rounded hills planted under vines, and the formal patterned squares of the peach and pear orchards. In the far distance the pale water-blue outline of Table Mountain and Devil's Peak.

It was cool in the shade of the trees and the water of the stream was cold and peaty. After lunch I stood at the edge of the cliff and looked over the ledge. The water fell down a sheer drop of forty feet on to a bed of smoothly rounded stones, flowing through them to form a deep dark pool. Halfway down the cliff a silvery-leafed *waboom* bearing two spiky lime green flowers grew from the solid rock face.

'I must climb down and hack that out sometime,' Johan said. 'It spoils the façade of the cliff; but I'm intrigued to see how long an arid loving plant will survive under such moist conditions.'

'Oh Johan!' Lynette cried. 'Won't it be dangerous?' She was enchantingly pretty.

I quickly glanced at him wondering if he'd noticed the nasal twang.

Later we scrambled down the precipitous path under the gnarled trees until we found ourselves in a glade on the edge of the dark pool, looking up at the slender waterfall and the dripping crag. The mossy rocks were bejewelled with hundreds of red disas – the most beautiful and opulent of South African orchids.

'Now you can see why it's called Wonderkloof,' Johan said quietly.

This, and many other memories enriched by childhood.

When Johan became an international rugby player

my mother and I watched every match played in Johannesburg and Pretoria. Trina came up from the Cape and always sat with us. She was a partisan vociferous spectator and often embarrassed me. We seldom watched a match without her becoming embroiled in an acrimonious argument. People turned around and stared, nudging each other and smiling. 'That's Johan de Villiers' mother.' He was now a famous fly half known for his cunning and courage.

When I left school I completed a course in bookkeeping, shorthand and typing and took a secretarial post with a small prosperous business in the centre of the city.

'Next year,' my mother said, 'we'll pay Charles and Elizabeth a visit.'

But the next year she died. She must have been ill for months. One day with frightening clarity I saw how thin and drawn she was – the dark shadows under her eyes emphasizing the transparent pallor of her skin. The cold hand of fear clutched me and I sprang to my feet crying out in the loud accusing tone of youth 'Mother you're sick!' Within three months she was dead. During the last dark days Trina stayed with me; small strong and comforting.

Now I was on my way to Wonderkloof to live with her. She'd flown down to the Cape two days ahead of me. On meeting me at the airport her welcome was matter-of-fact and brusque, knowing that a kind word or gesture of sympathy would make me cry. I was painfully vulnerable, unprepared for the shock, overwhelming grief and loneliness my mother's death was to bring.

As we neared Wonderkloof she laid her slim brown hand on my knee. 'I'm so glad you're coming to live with us Anna. I've always wanted a daughter.' The tears gushed into my eyes and I averted my face, staring fixedly out of the window. 'The boys are also delighted,' she continued as though she hadn't noticed. 'You'll be amazed how Pieter's grown since Christmas. He's nearly as tall as Johannes.'

I blew my nose and surreptitiously wiped my eyes. 'Will he be good at rugby like Johan?' I asked in a muffled voice.

She smiled. 'He certainly thinks so. Did I tell you that Johannes' rugby days are over?'

'No,' I said surprised. 'Why?'

'He injured his knee badly in the last Test against the Lions. The doctors say he'll never play again.'

'I'm sorry,' I murmured. 'Is he very disappointed?'

She swung the car too sharply (she was always an erratic driver) and turned into the oak avenue which stretched for a mile before reaching the gates of Wonderkloof. 'Not unduly so. It's just as well. Wonderkloof needs him. Johannes is a good farmer, but those trips overseas, and gallivanting all over the country kept him away from the farm too long.' She drove too fast over a bump and my handbag fell off my lap. 'Johannes has had six years of international rugby and it's time he settled down.'

We drove through the tall white gates of Wonderkloof, and for the first time in weeks I felt a tremor of happiness.

'The old apple-orchard's gone; we're putting it under vines. Johannes is planting them today, that's why he didn't come with me to meet you. He plants new vines every year and has modernized the cellar. We're now producing some of the best wine in the country.'

She slowed down at the drift with a grinding of gears. The stream, swollen from the winter rains was flowing strongly, the muddy water gurgling and lapping at the

wheels. Once we were through the poplar wood with its
sweet mouldy smell, I could see the rich newly tilled
earth where the apple-orchard had grown. I saw Johan's
tall khaki-clad figure standing amongst the *volk*, and he
lifted his hat and waved it as we drove past. We swept
around the bend and there was the square double-
storeyed old house with its small triangular central
pediment bearing the date 1792. The year Johan's great,
great grandfather built it for his young bride. It stood
white and serene behind the leafless oaks.

'Oh Trina!' I exclaimed in surprise. 'I didn't know
there were two urns on the roof.'

She nodded and smiled. 'Aren't they lovely? Of
course you haven't stayed at Wonderkloof in the winter.
The urns and cornices are hidden in the summer.' She
slowed down and stopped at the foot of the wide steps
leading up to the *stoep* and front door. 'And you haven't
seen Wonderkloof in the spring – the wild flowers, blossom and roses. To-morrow I'll teach you to prune. My
roses should have been done weeks ago.' She smiled.
'You'll be able to help me in so many ways, darling. I'm
sure you'll be happy with us.' I snatched my bag and
scrambled out of the car feeling an uprush of uncon-
trollable tears.

Upstairs I stood at the window of the bedroom, which
I'd shared with my mother, and looked down on Trina's
white-walled garden. Though winter was nearly over,
the deciduous trees were still leafless and fallen leaves
floated in the swimming-pool and carpeted the lawn,
but the sun was shining and at the west wall the almond
trees had their first sprinkling of blossom.

When I came into the sitting-room, the tea table
stood beside Trina's chair and Johan sat on the sofa in
front of the fire, his hands loosely clasped between his
long legs. He rose quickly when he saw me. I was tense;

19

frightened he'd say a word of sympathy and make me cry.

'Hallo Johan.' My voice sounded strained.

I needn't have worried.

He smiled warmly and kissed me on the cheek. 'Hallo Anna. Welcome Home!'

Chapter Two

JOHAN AND TRINA had started breakfast when I joined them in the dining-room the next morning. Trina's siamese cat Isabella, slept in the sun on the window-sill, amorphous and placid, and I paused to tickle her under the chin. She opened her blue eyes, stretched and yawned widely.

'She's just like Johannes' grandmother,' Trina said. 'All she ever thinks of is eating and sleeping.'

Johan had risen to wish me good-morning and raised his eyebrow as he sat down. His dog Wolf lay curled at his feet.

'Will you have porridge, my dear?'

'No thank-you.'

'Lettie!' she called, 'bring Miss Anna's eggs and bacon. Johannes, pass the butter to Anna.'

She sipped her coffee, looking at me over the rim of her cup. 'You should have seen what this old place looked like when I came to live here with Jan. The floors and furniture unpolished and the house so dirty I was ashamed.' She paused while Lettie placed a plate of bacon and eggs in front of me. 'The garden was a wilderness choked with weeds. Johannes' grandmother lay in bed all day and his grandfather was never here.' She raised her eyebrows enquiringly. 'You knew of course that his grandfather was Minister of Lands?' I nodded. 'The two of them let Wonderkloof go to rack and ruin. She never lifted a finger and before Jan's father died went to bed and stayed there for ten years. Ten years! Can you believe it? – and nothing wrong with her!' She drew the tray nearer and poured herself a second cup of coffee. 'She insisted on sleeping in my poor Jan's study instead of her own room upstairs so that she didn't miss anything. A bell stood next to her bed and a little coloured girl was constantly at her beck and call. Whenever she heard a sound she rang the bell, and the little girl ran to find out what had happened. If the dog barked or someone laughed loudly, she wanted to know why. Visitors were called in to entertain her, while she sat up in bed like a great blowzy rose.' She lit a cigarette and blew the smoke through her nostrils. 'The trays of food carried to that room! It wasn't only the regular meals – all day long she rang the bell, demanding cookies, *watermelon konfyt, mosbolletjies* – she stuffed herself from morning to night.' She clicked her tongue. 'I still get angry when I think about it.' She looked at Johan, her face severe. 'You see how important it is to marry the right girl.'

He looked up. 'Yes, Ma.' He caught my eye and winked.

'It's no laughing matter!' she said sharply. 'Your grandmother was a beautiful girl – and look what she turned out to be, a bone-idle woman! Too lazy to have more than one child – my poor Jan was a lonely, neglected little boy.'

'He was fond of her.'

'Of course he was fond of her,' she said impatiently. 'It wouldn't be natural for a boy not to love his mother.' She stubbed out her cigarette. 'She was a bad mother, and a bad wife! I'm always telling you Johannes, looks

22

aren't everything. It's also important that a girl can cook, sew and run your home.'

He grinned. 'Cooking and sewing isn't everything, Ma.'

'Nor's the other thing,' she said darkly.

'What other thing?' he asked innocently.

She reddened with annoyance. 'I wish you'd be serious, Johannes!'

He pushed his chair back. 'Well, I must be off,' he glanced at me. 'Are you coming?'

I jumped up with a light heart and followed him. He paused to pick up his hat from the stinkwood *rusbank* in the hall.

'Ma's not altogether right,' he said, as we walked down the steps. 'About *Ouma*, I mean. She forgot to tell you that *Oupa* was Minister of Lands for the shortest time on record. I think the government got rid of him on account of his lurid private life. He was a damned old roué, and finally brought his mistress to live at Wonderkloof. That's when poor old *Ouma* took to her bed. I remember her well. She was kind and jolly, and whenever I went to her room kissed me and gave me sweets. Ma's bitter because between them, *Oupa* and *Ouma* nearly ruined the family. For years she and Pa struggled to make ends meet – there was a time they were so much in debt they thought they might have to sell Wonderkloof. Fortunately Ma was able to borrow from her inheritance – invested in stocks and shares: this enabled them to weather the storm. That's why she periodically goes to Johannesburg.' He pulled a wry face. 'She's given me her power of attorney. Now I have to go.' He called Wolf to heel. 'There were times she drove my father very hard. She's an indomitable woman, Anna. She, more than anyone, is responsible for Wonderkloof being the prosperous farm it is today.

D'you know,' he stopped and looked at me, 'I've never seen her cry. Not even on the day Pa was killed.'

He pushed his hat off his forehead. 'From here we've one of the views of the farm I like most.'

We were standing on a ridge looking down on the neat pear and peach orchards and the softly rounded hills ribbed with vines. The course of the stream flowing through the farm was defined by the bullrushes, lush vegetation and great weeping-willows growing along its banks. A tall clump of bamboo stood near the darker green of the small olive orchard where in the past the slaves of Wonderkloof were buried.

Johan pointed and grinned. 'Look at the *volk*! I told them to meet me next to the slaves' grave-yard, but they're standing a quarter of a mile away – they're certain it's haunted.'

'I don't blame them.'

The grove of stunted barren olive trees, twisted and warped into grotesque shapes, smothered and dripping with rank creepers was a sinister place. The mounds of the graves were scattered haphazardly between the boles of the trees and not a leaf stirred in the strange green twilight.

We walked down the slope with Wolf at our heels. The *volk* lifted their disreputable hats as we approached. Adonis the foreman stood apart, insolently masculine, with the wide slack-lipped mouth of the drinker, and the bold stare of the womanizer.

'This morning,' Johan said, clearing his throat and looking at them individually, 'we're going to clean the slaves' graveyard, pull the creepers off the trees, fertilize them and weed the graves.'

Consternation and dismay was written on every brown face. A few even fell back a pace in horror.

24

The heavy silence was broken by Johan's delighted laughter.

They stared at him blankly, and then pandemonium broke loose. They howled. They slapped their knees and pointed at one another like children. They rolled on the ground holding their bellies. When I reached the top of the ridge I could still hear the joyful sound of their laughter.

I found Trina in the kitchen talking to Bella the cook. Trina was wearing a gardening smock brightly patterned with pink, red and purple poppies. Bella had been cook at Wonderkloof ever since I could remember. She was black-skinned and massive. She was also sanctimonious and self-righteous, her pendulous lips were invariably pursed in disapproval.

Trina picked up her gardening basket. 'Bella, tell Lettie I want her to make up the other bed in Miss Anna's room.' She turned to me, 'I forgot to tell you that I've invited Maria for the weekend. You're fond of each other and it will be good for you to have company.'

In the hall she put her gardening basket on the yellow-wood and stinkwood table next to the window overlooking the court-yard and opened the drawer taking out two dusting-cloths. 'First of all, we'll do a little dusting. There are pieces of china and glass I don't allow the servants to touch.' She ran her dusting-cloth over the front of the marquetry grandfather clock. 'Maria will come with Julian this evening. He and Johannes are gallivanting as usual tonight. It's high time those two men settled down. They're twenty-six and think of nothing but parties and girls.' She lifted a heavy brown jar and lovingly polished its bright glaze. 'Look at this martavanen jar, Anna. It dates back to the Ming period. I keep telling Johannes he's wearing himself out. He's up at dawn, works hard all day, and then goes out and comes home in the small hours of the morning. I wish he'd settle down, and start a family. Last month I invited such a charming girl to spend the weekend. Johannes hardly opened his mouth and never addressed a word to her. At times he's very pig-headed.' She stood on her toes and removed a hexagonal vase from the gueridon. 'Look at this Imari vase. There's probably not another one like it in the country. Look at the herons and flowers, like peonies. It should be in a museum or locked away in a cabinet with the Nanking china. There was an even finer one which was broken before I came to Wonderkloof. Oh! All the things that were broken and stolen while Johannes' grandmother lay in bed. I mustn't allow myself to think about it!' She gazed with affection at the magnificent stinkwood cabinet, filled with Nanking willow-pattern china, and gently dusted the yellow-wood panels and the finely carved gabled pediment. 'Just look at the silver key plates! Absolutely black! I told Lettie to polish them yesterday. She's lazy and insolent. I'd like to get rid of her, but I know Bella will leave if I do. Lettie's her youngest and the apple of her eye. Bella spoils her but keeps her on too tight a rein, and the child becomes frustrated. That's what the quarrelling was about this morning. Didn't you hear the screaming and shouting coming from the kitchen? I had to go in and stop them. I often wonder who Lettie's father was – she was born three years after Bella's husband left her. Her other children are as black-skinned as she is.'

Lettie was golden-brown. The skin on her flat cheekbones gleamed like silk. Her body was ripe and her mouth full and sulky. I didn't like her. Her eyes were insolent and her manner sullen and familiar.

Trina took my dusting-cloth and put it back in the drawer, shutting it with a bang. She picked up her gardening basket and we walked through Johan's study to

26

the garden. Her gardening hat was hanging behind the door and she clapped it on tying it under her chin. 'Come, Anna. I'll initiate you into the joys and ardour of pruning.'

Trina and I were sitting in front of the fire in the sitting-room when Julian and Maria arrived. I jumped up and kissed Maria, knowing she wouldn't mention my mother or say anything sympathetic to undermine my self-control.

Trina kissed her affectionately and patted the sofa. 'Sit next to me, dear child. How's your mother?'

'She's very well *Tant'* Trina, and sends her love.'

Her brother Julian and Johan came in. Julian kissed Trina's cheek. 'Good-evening *Tant'* Trina.'

'Good-evening Julian,' she said coolly.

He shook hands with me. 'Good-evening Anna.'

I was never at ease with him. He made me feel young, gauche and unattractive. He was dark and handsome with a clefted chin, a fine classical nose and large long-lashed brown eyes. He was infinitely aware of his good looks.

Trina's chilly reception disconcerted him and made him ill at ease. He loosened his collar and looked at his watch. 'We must be going Johan. We're supposed to be there at eight.'

'Where are you going, Johannes?' Trina asked.

He smiled amiably. 'Out, Ma,' he said firmly.

She moved irritably and clicked her tongue. As he leaned down to kiss her she reached up a small brown hand and ruffled his hair.

'It's funny,' Maria said, when they'd gone. 'Julian's really handsome yet he hasn't half Johan's sex-appeal.'

'Sex-appeal!' Trina cried in a loud contemptuous voice.

27

Maria grinned and her brown eyes sparkled. 'It's true, *Tant*' Trina! He has oodles of it.'

Trina shuddered. 'What dreadful expressions you young people use.'

'He has a lean and hungry look. Don't you agree, Anna?' She winked at me and suppressed a giggle.

'Johannes is an ordinary healthy good-looking boy!' Trina said angrily. 'Who should be thinking of settling down, instead of gallivanting with that brother of yours. Come, children,' she stood up. 'I heard the bell. Let's go in to dinner.' Wolf slipped like a shadow into the room and lay down next to Johan's chair. 'He's an unsatisfactory animal,' Trina said, as we walked through the hall. 'Nobody exists for him except Johannes. He ignores me though he sees me every day, and backs away if I try to stroke him. I keep telling Johannes that a dog should be friends with everyone in the house.'

'What kind of dog is he, *Tant*' Trina?'

'A Norwegian Elkhound. Given to him,' she added grimly, 'by an admirer.'

Chapter Three

WE TOOK THREE days to prune the roses. Trina was a slavedriver and never tired.

Winter blew itself out in a final north-west gale, which uprooted one of the old pear trees growing against the east wall of her garden.

She crooned and mourned over it, running her hand over the smooth trunk. 'It was here when I came to Wonderkloof as a young bride. Even then, it was old and barren, but every spring it was white with blossom. Look, Anna, you can see the buds, in another ten days it would have been in blossom. I feel as though I've lost an old friend.' All day she was silent and depressed.

The next morning she poured the coffee and handed Johan's cup to him. 'Johannes, you must tell Adonis to bring a couple of boys here this evening. I want them to chop up the old pear tree. It will make good firewood for the next winter.' She passed him the sugar. 'Bella told me this morning that Adonis thrashed his wife again on Friday night. She says he gave her a black eye and knocked out one of her front teeth. You must speak to him, Johannes!'

He glanced up. 'Ma, I'm always speaking to him. You know as well as I do what happens. The *volk* get drunk on Friday nights and half the time they don't know what they're doing.'

'You must speak to him again!' she cried peremptorily. She turned to me. 'D'you remember, when Adonis married Annekie six years ago at Christmas? She was small and slim, with a little round face and soft velvety eyes like a buck.' She paused. 'If you saw her now you wouldn't know her. She's cowed and broken. Her front teeth are gone – I was surprised to hear from Bella that there were any left to knock out, and the poor child is permanently pregnant. Not only that!' Her voice rose with indignation. 'He also fathers more than half the illegitimate babies on this farm – and the farm next door as well! Bettie tells me he's always skulking around their backyard.' She looked at Johan again. 'You must speak to him Johannes!'

He pushed his cup away. 'Ma,' he said quietly. 'I've told you before that I've spoken to him. He appears penitent, but it makes no difference.'

'We should get rid of him!' she cried angrily.

'Look, Ma,' he said impatiently. 'You know as well as I do, that Adonis is the best foreman in the district and we're damned lucky to have him.'

'Don't swear at me, Johannes!'

'I'm not swearing at you,' he said mildly. 'I'm merely stressing my point.' He got up. 'I must be going.' As he went out of the room he looked over his shoulder. 'Are you coming, Anna?'

When I returned I found Trina waiting for me in the hall. 'I thought we'd go to the *volks'* cottages and see how Annekie is. The poor child is expecting again.' She picked up a basket covered with a white napkin. 'I'm taking a few things for her and the children.'

She opened the barn-door which led into the courtyard. The assortment of pot-plants, begonias and ferns growing in tubs and pots against the walls always fascinated me and I stopped to look at them. She stood next to me and took my arm. 'You may look after the pot-plants for me – I always forget to feed them. If you look in the shed behind the dairy you'll find fertilizer. Feed them once a fortnight and you'll have a wonderful reward.' She smiled. 'And you'll also be doing me a service.'

I opened the gate leading on to the farm-yard. The old oak next to the packing-shed was bursting into leaf – the massive trunk stood practically horizontal; a wooden box was hidden in the branches in which some of the scrawny hens laid eggs – it was easy to walk along the trunk and collect them.

Fowls, ducks and geese wandered between the homestead and the packing-sheds. Bella fed them each morning and evening. When they heard her strange high-pitched cry 'Kip! Kip! Kip! Kip!', they'd appear from every direction – wings flapping, scraggy necks stretched out, running, flying and cackling. Every evening I took a basket and collected the eggs.

A cold blustery wind buffeted us and the sky was dark and lowering. The *volks'* cottages stood in a straggling row, the stream which flowed behind them hidden by a tall bank of oaks. As we approached I smelt the familiar pungent wood-smoke which I always associate with the *volk* – the rank smell of sweat and smoke was as much part of them as their clothing. We were surrounded and followed by a horde of small coloured children. Their jerseys were too small, filthy and full of holes. The smallest were naked from below the waist. In the summer their faces would be crawling with flies. A couple of emaciated dogs barked at us, tails between their legs, and a half-starved cat fled into the bush.

The coloured women greeted us respectfully and

remained in their doorways, watching us inquisitively as we walked to Annekie's cottage. Hearing the dogs bark and the sound of voices, she appeared at the entrance, two small children clinging to her skirts. She wore a faded, stained and filthy dress, tightly strained over her swollen belly. Her two frightened half-naked children, looking dirty and under-nourished.

'Good-morning, Annekie.'

'Good-morning, *Ou Nooi*,' she said in a low hoarse voice, dropping her eyes.

Trina was right – I wouldn't have recognized her. Her nose was broken and her face scarred, ravaged and coarsened. Her left eye was closed and her swollen mouth raw and bleeding. But most horrifying of all was her apathy.

Trina and I were silent on the way home. As we entered the court-yard she clasped my arm. 'The irony of it is – she probably still loves him.'

That evening when I returned to the house with my basket of eggs, I saw Adonis talking to Lettie at the kitchen door. She stood close to him looking demurely at the ground, a faint smile curving her sulky mouth. He was leaning against the wall of the house, his jacket slung over his shoulder and a wide smile on his loose-lipped mouth as he looked down the front of her dress.

At that moment Bella's immense figure loomed in the doorway. She seized Lettie by the elbow and with one heave of her brawny arm, jerked her into the passage and hit her across the face. Lettie gave a piercing shriek and I heard her run down the passage, crying hysterically.

Bella reappeared in the doorway. 'What you doing here, you dirty *hotnot*!' she cried shrilly. She leaned back and armed herself with a broom, her pendulous lips trembling with rage. 'You keep away from my Lettie. D'you hear! You good-for-nothing dirty *skelm*!'

He put his hand on his hip, and looked her up and down with studied insolence.

'Go on!' she shouted, her voice rising. 'You get away from her, you *vabond*! *Voetsak*!'

He grinned and said two unprintable words, then turned on his heel and sauntered away, whistling loudly while she stood in the doorway shouting obscenities until he disappeared around the corner.

Trina wanted me to spend the weekend with Maria at their farm Mooi Vlei, but I stubbornly refused. Maria and I had been friends since we were children, and I was fond of her, but her mother, *Tant'* Bettie, was a sentimental, emotional woman, whom I knew would say something about my mother and make me cry. I was also nervous of her father, *Oom* Gert, who was notorious for his weakness for women. His ogling eyes embarrassed me and I was constantly avoiding his pawing hands.

Now Trina was taking me to spend the day with Maria. When she stopped in front of the thatch-roofed, gabled homestead, she sensed my tension and patted my knee. 'I'll tell Johannes to fetch you at six o'clock.'

Maria and *Tant'* Bettie appeared at the front door to greet me. *Tant'* Bettie's blue eyes were drenched in tears and she clasped me with emotion to her bosom. '*Ag*, my dear child, my poor little Anna.'

I burst into tears.

'Oh Mom!' Maria exclaimed impatiently. She took my arm and held it firmly. 'Come. We'll see you later, Mom. I'm taking Anna to meet Martin.' She continued to grip my arm as we walked down the hall. I stopped to grope in my bag for a handkerchief and wiped my eyes and blew my nose. 'Mom's the bottom!'

She opened the barn-door and we stepped on to the

stoep. A young man was reclining on the swing-seat and rose quickly as we came through the doorway.

'Anna, I don't think you've met Martin Joubert.'

We shook hands and I hastily wiped away the last tears.

We spent the day wandering over the farm. The fruit trees were coming into blossom and the ground was carpeted with yellow sorrels. Mooi Vlei adjoined Wonderkloof and I could see the square homestead in the distance. The high peaks were brilliantly blue and the green gash of the *kloof* was clearly visible.

'I've heard about the *kloof*,' Martin looked up at the peaks. 'Will you take me to see it one day, Anna?' He was quiet, sensitive and shy.

We saw Johan driving up the oak avenue and walked to the car to meet him.

Martin opened the door for me. 'May I see you soon?' I nodded, smiling as shyly as he did.

A moment later Maria darted forward and put her fair head through the window, her brown eyes sparkling mischievously. 'You've made a conquest,' she said in a stage whisper, grinning like an urchin.

Johan lifted his brows humorously, turned the car and we waved to them as we drove off. 'Well, how did you enjoy your day?'

'I enjoyed it more than I expected – I was dreading it! You know what *Tant'* Bettie's like.'

'Did *Oom* Gert pinch your bottom?'

'He wasn't there, thank goodness! He and Julian went to Cape Town for the day. Anyway,' I added, 'he's not so bad with me as he is with most girls. I don't think I have the sort of bottom that gets pinched.'

He looked at me sideways with a little smile. 'Don't underestimate yourself Anna.'

Chapter Four

'JOHANNES,' Trina said at breakfast a few weeks later, 'I was walking past the family grave-yard yesterday afternoon and noticed that the wall needs mending. You and Pieter must do something about it next week when he gets back from school.' She turned to me, 'You know the grave-yard on the hill – the low white wall with the corrugated iron roof? Johannes and I will be buried there one day.' I involuntarily winced, and she continued as though she hadn't noticed. 'When Johannes was eighteen the wall needed mending so he arranged for the *volk* to meet him there at eight o'clock in the morning. He arrived an hour early and removed some of the bricks, making a big enough hole to climb into the tomb. He waited until the *volk* were all there and then suddenly banged on the roof. They got such a fright they dropped their tools and fled and haven't been within a mile of the place since.' She laughed loudly. 'He had to mend it himself and carry their tools home.' She paused and grinned with grim satisfaction. 'He's had to mend it ever since.'

'Ma always enjoys that part of the story,' Johan said in a dry voice.

She felt in her pocket and took out her cigarette case. 'You'll be twenty-one next week, Anna.'

'Yes, on the fifteenth of September.'

'I would like to have given a dance for you at Wonderkloof.'

'No.' I said quickly.

'I know, darling,' she said gently, laying her hand on mine. 'We won't have a dance this year – but perhaps next year when you turn twenty-two. Tomorrow we'll drive to Cape Town to fetch Pieter. He'll be so pleased to see you.'

That morning Johan and I walked down the paddock towards the poplar wood. 'This is the paddock where the horses used to graze. Did you know that Ma was a magnificent horsewoman?'

'I can believe it,' I said, thinking of her slim wiry body and small strong hands.

'She and Pa rode for miles over the farm every day. I'd my own horse and Pieter rode when he was three.' He whistled to Wolf and paused to fondle his head. 'She never liked the stallion Pa bought. He was a vicious bad-tempered brute but Pa loved him. She was always at him to get rid of the animal – you know how she can go on: but Pa could be very obstinate. She always told him he was pigheaded.' He paused. 'The day Pa was killed I knew something had happened when I saw the stallion galloping to the stables in a sweat. Adonis and I went to look for him and found him lying at the edge of the poplar wood.' His face tightened. 'We found what was left of him after the stallion had thrown and trampled him. We carried him to the house and Ma met us in the hall. I'll always remember how straight she stood when she saw us coming through the front door, and how quietly she said "Take him upstairs Johannes and put him on his bed." Later she went to the stables and shot the stallion herself. She sold every horse on the farm. I told you she didn't cry after Pa was killed – except for

36

getting rid of the horses, she remained exactly the same.' He stopped and picked up a stick while Wolf watched him, and tapped it in the palm of his hand. 'Sometimes I think it would have been better for her if she'd cried.'

'Of course she cried,' I said quietly. 'She cried when she was alone in the deep dark hours of the night.' He looked at me quickly, and I flushed and turned away. 'I must go to her, she'll wonder where I am.'

She was in the garden disbudding the roses. Spring had started. The crab apple was a feathery cloud of pink and white blossom and scarlet buds. The transparent bronze leaves of the copper beech were unfurling, and the delicate lace-like foliage of the Japanese Maple stirred and whispered in the breeze.

'Johannes' great grandmother started this garden,' Trina said. 'She was an Englishwoman who came from Bath. Her name was Gertrude Barton, the daughter of a wealthy merchant who came to settle in the Cape. She met Pierre de Villiers and married him the following year.' She continued disbudding the roses. 'She was a remarkable woman of discriminating taste. She planted the copper beech, the rhododendrons, azaleas and pink magnolia tree, and bought the carved marble bench in Florence.' She watched critically as I disbudded. 'That's right, Anna – but you're too slow.' Her small hands fluttered mothlike from one rose bush to another. 'Gertrude de Villiers did more for Wonderkloof than any member of the family.'

'Johan says that about you.'

Her face softened. 'Have you noticed how much Johannes resembles her? You must know her portrait in the dining-room. He's inherited her narrow face, grey eyes and rather prominent chin. Her face was too severe for beauty, but she was a fine handsome woman.'

Lettie appeared at the study door and slowly crossed the lawn carrying the tea tray. She placed it on the white table underneath the magnolia tree with a resounding crash.

'Oh! How I wish I could get rid of that girl,' Trina muttered angrily. 'She casts a gloom over the house. She and Bella are either not on speaking terms or having a screaming contest.'

We drank our tea in the shade of the magnolia tree with its chaliced blooms, the lawn at our feet carpeted with thick pink petals.

That afternoon I walked half-way up the mountain, searching in the *veld* for the delicate pink *pypie* which Trina told me flowered at Wonderkloof in the spring. This dainty wild gladioli could only be found on the upper slopes of the farm.

It was nearly six o'clock when I returned, and I met Johan as he was leaving the packing-sheds. He held out his hand and took my bunch of flowers. 'I remember picking these for Ma when I was a little boy. She'll be delighted.'

We crossed the farm-yard and saw Adonis talking to Lettie next to the bent oak. She was looking up at him, standing in the circle of his arms. As we approached, his hands moved down and caressed her buttocks. She turned and saw us, slipped quickly from his grasp and ran down to the house. Without looking at us he picked up his jacket and sauntered nonchalantly towards the *volks'* cottages.

'Damn that boy!' Johan muttered. 'I'll have to speak to him again – not that it will make the slightest difference. Don't tell Ma, Anna – you know how she'll go on.' He walked as far as the tree and pushed his hat back. 'Adonis!' he shouted. 'Come here!' I left him and walked down to the house. I heard him say angrily,

'I'm warning you for the last time. Leave that girl alone!'

I found Trina in the sitting-room. When she saw me she stretched out both hands and took my bunch of flowers as though I were handing her priceless pearls.

Lettie came into my bedroom the next morning without knocking.

'Lettie, you must knock when you come into my room.'

'I sorry, Miss Anna. I forget.' Her soft full lips curved in an unaccustomed, ingratiating smile, and she looked at me uneasily, dropping her eyes. 'Miss Anna won't tell Bella you see me talking to Adonis?'

'Why should I? It isn't my business.' Then I said impulsively, 'Lettie, why are you such a fool? Why d'you play around with a bad man like Adonis? It can only get you into trouble. Don't you know what he's like!'

She glared at me with angry insolence. 'I not play around with Adonis!' she cried shrilly. 'I not play around with married men. I respectable – what sort of girl you think I am!' Her voice rose hysterically. 'You think a respectable girl like me play around with dirt like Adonis? You think I bad rubbish!'

'All right Lettie, that's enough! You may go.'

She traced the pattern on the carpet with her toe and lowered her voice. 'I only talking to him, Miss Anna. If Bella know I talk to him it make big troubles.'

'I've already told you I won't tell her.'

She smiled placatingly as she softly closed the door.

On my way to breakfast I looked through the case-ment windows of the upper hall and saw that the trellised old vine was in leaf; the crinkled new leaves were burnished iridescent green-gold in the sun.

39

Later that morning Trina and I drove to Cape Town to fetch Pieter. It was a sparkling spring day. Fat clumps of arum lilies dotted the green fields and grew along the sides of the road. On the Cape Flats the yellow wattle was in bloom, and the banks of the white sand-dunes were bejewelled with glittering *vygies* and fringed with tall cyclamen-coloured daisies. Yellow and white daisies were scattered like stardust on the fields and on the edge of the road. In the distance we saw the outline of Table Mountain and Devil's Peak; at first small and palely blue, but darkening and enlarging as we approached the outskirts of the city.

'How I love that mountain!' Trina said, her voice deepening. 'It's so big, friendly and protective.' She swung the car too sharply and I fell against her. 'I've only seen one other mountain that moves me as much – the soaring Matterhorn.' She took her eye from the road to look at me. 'It's beautiful, Anna! Slender, ethereal and majestic like the spire of a cathedral.' She skidded round the corner and turned into the school gates. 'One day we must go to Zermatt and see it.'

We were late and Pieter was waiting. He looked tall and lanky in his school clothes and smiled when he saw us.

He kissed Trina. 'Gee, Ma. You're late!' He came around to the other window. 'Hello, Anna.' Unlike his brother, he kissed me full on the mouth.

'Anna,' Trina said during dinner. 'Johannes and I agree that it would be a good idea for you to help us with the books, and type our business letters. Now, I type them rather badly with one finger.'

'It's a good idea,' Johan said. 'Also,' he added with a grin, 'you'll be taking Ma off my back.'

Pieter guffawed and Trina's eyebrows twitched with

40

annoyance. 'There's something else I want to discuss with you. Our nextdoor neighbour Colonel Jamieson, has returned from his trip to the Far East, and I—'

'Ma's old boyfriend,' Johan interrupted.

Pieter's bellow of oafish laughter was deafening. She frowned, 'Your laugh sounds like the bray of a donkey.'

'Gee, Ma,' he looked hurt. 'You're always picking on me.'

'As I was saying, Colonel Jamieson's back. He writes rather dull travel books.' She seized Pieter's elbow and banged it on the table. 'For the hundredth time – take your elbows off the table!'

'Gee, Ma.'

'He has endless trouble finding someone to type his books and do a little secretarial work. I mentioned your name and he was very interested. How d'you feel about it? You'll have to go to him twice a week, and could type his book in your spare time. I'll see to it that he pays you well.'

'I think it's a wonderful idea.'

'Good,' she smiled. 'I'll arrange it when he dines with us next week. Johannes, I've invited him to dinner and bridge on Thursday night. I hope you'll be here.'

He looked up. 'I'll be here, but I want to be in bed by half past ten.'

She sniffed loudly. 'When you're out to all hours of the night with those girls – d'you tell them you want to be in bed by half past ten?'

He leered at her. 'What are you suggesting, Ma?'

'Johannes! Remember your younger brother is present!'

Pieter winked at me and grinned.

She rang the bell for Lettie to clear away the plates. 'I've also invited Bettie and Gert, and the couple who have bought the van Ryn's farm – that rather dull man with the good-looking wife. I only hope Gert wi.. behave himself.' She looked at me. 'You'll have to play bridge, Anna.'

'Oh!' I exclaimed. 'I'm very bad.'

'You won't be any worse than the rest of them. Did you know that your father played an excellent game of bridge? Your poor dear mother on the other hand—' She checked herself.

I managed to smile. 'Yes, Mom had no confidence, she always dithered and wondered what her partner wanted her to do.'

This was the first time I'd voluntarily mentioned my mother's name since her death, and I felt happier, as though she were closer to me. I remembered her at the bridge table fingering first one card and then another, moving uneasily, an anxious frown knitting her brows.

Trina lifted her glass to me and smiled.

Chapter Five

OU CHRISTIAAN and *Ou* Attie had worked in Trina's garden for nearly thirty years. *Ou* Attie was black-skinned, negroid and morose. I'd never seen him smile, nor did he speak unless spoken to. *Ou* Christiaan's Hottentot ancestry was apparent in his flat-nosed, yellowish-brown face, toothless and wrinkled like an old apple. They wore incongruous cast-off hats of Trina's. She scolded and bullied them unmercifully and always complained of their laziness and arrant stupidity.

Ou Christiaan was cheerful and as inquisitive as a monkey. He was intrigued to see me feeding the ferns and begonias in the court-yard and stood watching where Trina couldn't see him. 'Why don't *Klein Nooi* plant fuschias in pots? (he always called me "little mistress".) They grow well here in the shade. *Ou Nooi* make me plant slips – now they grow and *Ou Nooi* forget.'

I searched in the shed behind the dairy and found a stack of earthenware pots. Pieter helped me carry them to the court-yard, then pushed a wheelbarrow to the oak forest beyond the garden and came back with a load of humus and leafmould.

He had Trina's dark brown eyes, but otherwise was the image of his father and had inherited his unfailing good humour.

We filled the pots and carefully planted and watered the slips. When we'd finished we called Trina and showed her the results of our labour.

The 'phone rang and I heard Lettie answer. A moment later she came into the court-yard and smiled at me knowingly. 'There's a *baas* for Miss Anna on the 'phone.' Trina's head jerked up. When I came back I knelt and rearranged the pots. 'Help me with this one, Pieter. I think it will look better at the back.'

'Who was it?' Trina asked, unable to contain herself any longer.

'Martin Joubert – he's a friend of Maria's. He's asked me out on Wednesday night.'

'Oh.' It sounded like a pebble dropped into a still pool. 'I wonder if he's a son of Martin Joubert from Tulbagh?'

'I've no idea.'

'I must remember to ask Bettie some time.'

The next day was my birthday. Trina and Pieter came to my room while I was still in bed to give me their presents.

'Trina!' I exclaimed. 'A typewriter! What a wonderful present.'

'It will be useful, darling.' She was sitting on the edge of my bed and ran her hand through my hair.

Pieter waited with obvious impatience for me to unwrap his present.

'Perfume! Thank you, Pieter!'

He grinned engagingly. 'It's real snazzy stuff. They say it makes the hair curl on the men's chests.'

'Where d'you learn such vulgar expressions?' Trina muttered.

We'd almost finished breakfast when Johan came into the dining-room. He kissed Trina then came over and kissed my cheek. 'Good-morning, Anna. Happy

Birthday. I've a present for you in the study.' I leapt excitedly to my feet.

'Finish your breakfast Anna!' Trina said impatiently.

'Gee, Ma, be a sport! Let's see what Johan's got for her.' We trooped out of the dining-room with Trina on our heels.

Johan opened the study door and at first I didn't see anything; then a movement made me look at the floor next to the window, and I saw a small puppy lying in the sun, his hindlegs stretched out. He wagged his feathery tail and regarded me with a pair of friendly bulging eyes. His pushed-in nose was the size of a show button and his black face hideous and ludicrously human. With a cry I knelt and gathered him in my arms and he squirmed affectionately, snuffling and licking my face.

'His name is Chiang,' Johan said. 'He's a miniature pekinese – a very small model. Don't make a lapdog of him, Anna. You'll find him tough and courageous and when he's older he'll be able to follow you everywhere.' He looked at me and smiled warmly. 'Someone to keep you company in the deep dark hours of the night,' he added softly.

'What's that? What's that?' Trina asked in a loud voice.

'Nothing, Ma. Let's go and finish breakfast.'

I put Chiang on the floor and he followed us briskly to the dining-room. Isabella, the siamese cat, was cleaning herself on the window-sill. She stopped with her hindleg pointing upwards and stared at him. Her ears flattened and her eyes dilated, then she jumped to the floor with a heavy thump, her fur on end. Chiang was delighted and ran to her wagging his tail. She arched her back, spat and fled under the table.

'Be careful she doesn't scratch his eyes,' Trina warned.

He ran to Wolf and licked his face. Wolf froze and averted his head looking dangerous and showed the whites of his eyes. 'No, Wolf,' Johan said sternly, fondling his ears. 'Don't worry, Anna. They'll both accept him in time.'

Within a week Isabella doted on him. As soon as Chiang came into the room she jumped off the window-sill and greeted him with a miaow. She became sportive and playful. She hid under the furniture with only her black nose and squinting blue eyes visible, pouncing on him as he walked past. Tail erect, she followed him into the garden, hiding behind the shrubs and darting at him playfully. She lay with him on the sofa and industriously washed him. Sometimes she was rough, seizing him in a feline grip and burying her fangs in his soft throat, fiercely kicking him with her hindlegs. Then he yelped shrilly, and when she released him attacked her, barking and biting in a rage. 'I've never seen such a transformation in a cat,' Trina said. D'you remember what a dull pudding she used to be?'

'Perhaps that's what poor old *Ouma* needed,' Johan said. 'Just a little love and companionship.'

'Your grandmother was a bone idle woman!' she snapped.

But Wolf remained detached and withdrawn, ignoring all Chiang's overtures.

The day after my birthday we were reading in the sitting-room before dinner. Trina put her book on her lap and removed her spectacles. 'Sometime I'd like to invite the Malans and their daughter to spend the weekend,' she said to the room in general. 'D'you remember her, Johannes?' she asked affably.

He looked up from his book. 'If you invite that girl to this house,' he said in a louder voice than usual, 'I'll not be here.'

Pieter snickered and they both stared at him coldly.

'What have you against her, Johannes? She's charming.'

'I've no doubt.'

She turned to me. 'I was so impressed with her. You'll like her, Anna.'

'I hope she and Anna enjoy each other's company.'

'You're pigheaded, Johannes.'

'Yes, Ma.'

He closed his book and put it on the table. 'Now, if you'll excuse me, I'll go and get dressed.'

'Where are you going?'

'Out.'

'But you told me you'd be in for dinner!' she cried, in a loud accusing tone.

'I've changed my mind.'

She sighed loudly when he had gone. 'Johannes is a very obstinate man,' she said, shaking her head.

While we were having dinner I looked up and saw Johan walking through the hall towards the front door. His hair was combed, his lean chin smoothly shaven and he was wearing what Maria called his 'courting clothes'.

The next morning while we were having breakfast the door flew open and Maria burst unceremoniously into the room, face flushed and eyes shining with excitement. 'You'll never guess what's happened – I'm engaged!'

'Maria! Congratulations!' I cried, jumping up and kissing her. 'Is it John?'

'Yes,' she nodded, her face glowing.

'John? John who?' Trina asked.

'John Graham, *Tant'* Trina.'

'Graham?' Trina said, looking at the ceiling. Then she smiled and opened her arms. 'Congratulations, my child. Come and kiss me!'

Johan and Pieter kissed her, then she sat next to me. 'Oh, *tant*' Trina, I'm so excited. And Mom's so happy, she's been in floods of tears. We're having a small engagement party tonight to which you're all invited. Martin said he'd fetch you, Anna, and Johan, I hope you'll come, and bring a partner with you.'

'Why can't Johannes take Anna?' Trina said sharply. 'It isn't necessary for Martin to fetch her.'

'I want him to fetch me,' I said quickly.

When we arrived at Mooi Vlei that evening the party was in full swing and we had to push our way through the guests to find Maria. She was radiant. 'Look at Mom,' she whispered. 'She hasn't stopped dabbing her eyes since the first guest arrived.'

I looked at *Tant*' Bettie and saw her blowing her nose and watching *Oom* Gert who was laughing loudly, his face red and his arms around the slim waists of two of Maria's friends.

But what I remember most that night isn't Maria's radiance or *Tant*' Bettie's tears. It isn't *Oom* Gert's red face and booming laugh, or Julian arrogantly handsome, leaning against the wall watching the dancers, nor Martin holding my hand during the drive back to Wonderkloof.

It is the moment Maria nudged me and whispered, 'Look, there's Johan's girl-friend. He's been taking her out for nearly a year.'

They were standing at the window. She was white skinned with smooth auburn hair and so small she barely reached his shoulder. I saw her turn and speak to him and he looked down and smiled, putting his arm around her waist.

A hot searing flame of jealousy pierced me like an arrow.

Chapter Six

PIETER WAS THE only one at Wonderkloof who could make Bella smile. For him, the pursued pendulous lips unfolded with surprising sweetness. She called him 'my *Klein Baas*', (my little master). She upbraided Lettie if his shirts were badly washed or not well ironed. She stood in the doorway and called him in to offer him tidbits. He was welcome at all hours to come into her kitchen and demand food; and while he ate, he talked and made her laugh.

He was returning to school on Sunday. On Saturday, she spent the day baking cakes and cookies for his tuckbox. She took hours to ice a fruit cake, and beamed with pride when he complimented her. The next day when he came to say goodbye in his school clothes, her lips trembled and she wiped her eyes with the corner of her apron.

Trina and I drove him to Cape Town. During the trip he was silent and unresponsive, and when we arrived at the school he clambered out, kissed us avoiding our eyes, and walked away without looking back.

'Poor Pieter,' Trina sighed. 'He hates boarding-school so much! It nearly breaks his heart each time he has to leave Wonderkloof. Particularly now he's older and spends so much time helping Johannes on the farm.

D'you know,' she said, looking at me with a little smile. 'He was actually trying to persuade me to let him leave school when he turns sixteen. I told him I wouldn't even consider it! He must have the same education Johannes had. There's room for both of them at Wonderkloof: but he must go to University and take an agricultural degree.' She took the corner too fast and the tyres screamed as the car heeled. 'He has such a sweet nature – however cross and bad-tempered I am he never resents it. He'll always give me a kiss and hug and bears no ill will. I find him more affectionate than Johannes was at that age.' She felt in her bag and took out her cigarette case. 'Light me a cigarette, Anna.' I lit one and she took it without taking her eyes off the road. 'It hasn't been easy bringing up the boys. Johannes was seventeen when his father was killed, and Pieter only six. They've missed a man's firm handling. Johannes has always been stubborn. He's a good son and a good farmer, but I wish he'd settle down. His father was married at his age – with a son.' We drove in silence for a while. 'This boy you're going out with, Anna – this Martin Joubert. Is he the son of Martin Joubert from Tulbagh?'

'I haven't asked him.'

'Oh. I must remember to enquire sometime. Invite him to dinner one evening.'

'Yes, I will.' I touched her arm. 'Look at the mountain!' The high peaks behind Wonderkloof were mauve, purple and deep violet in the fading light.

The weather was hotter the next day and when I helped Trina in the garden I wore one of her bright straw hats. She was planning her herbaceous border. *Ou* Christiaan and *Ou* Attie were composting and digging over the long curved bed while she stood and watched them. 'This should have been done weeks ago.' There was great rivalry between Trina and *Tant'* Bettie. They planned their borders in secret. 'I've sown salpiglossis this year, and managed to get excellent seed. I know Bettie will be green with envy.' While we strolled around the garden she stopped every few minutes to pull out a weed. 'Last year she had the most beautiful perennial phlox – I've never seen such heads! D'you know, Anna, she wouldn't give me a single plant this year – not one! And when I asked her where she'd bought them she said she couldn't remember.' She stopped and looked around the garden. 'Where's Christiaan? Where's that wretched man? I've never known anyone so lazy!' She cupped her hands to her mouth. 'Christiaan!' she shouted loudly.

'Yes, *Ou Nooi*.' He came shuffling through the door in the high wall which hid the vegetable garden, holding a wooden tray.

'Where have you been?'

He beamed holding out his wooden box. 'I pick the first strawberries *Ou Nooi*. Look how big they is.'

'I told you to dig the bed over, not pick strawberries!' she said angrily.

His face fell. 'I sorry, *Ou Nooi*.'

'And why didn't you pick them while Master Pieter was here? You know how much he likes them.'

'I sorry, *Ou Nooi*,' he said again. He placed the strawberries in the shade and walked slowly to the border and picked up his spade.

Lettie came across the lawn carrying the tea tray. She placed it on the garden bench while she brushed the thick pink petals off the table. Trina and I watched her walking back to the house.

'I doubt if that child wears a stitch of clothing underneath her uniform! Am I imagining it, or have you also noticed that she seems less sulky?'

'I've noticed that she and Bella aren't quarrelling so much.'

51

Chiang was lying in one of the garden chairs in Isabella's arms. I picked him up and put him on my lap. He was as relaxed as a rag doll. I turned him on his back and he lay with his paws in the air and closed his eyes. Isabella jumped off the chair and miaowed for milk.

'What a lovely day,' Trina said. 'We're going to have a hot, early summer. I must 'phone tomorrow and make arrangements to have the swimming-pool painted. Attie always looks after the pool and keeps it clean. He's surly and moody but I find him more reliable than Christiaan.'

Johan was away for the day and shortly before twelve Trina left to have lunch at Somerset West. I stood on the *stoep* with Chiang in my arms and waved to her, watching the car until it disappeared in a cloud of dust around the bend.

I had an early lunch and then took Chiang for a walk along the shady path leading to the oak forest beyond the garden. It was cool, silent and peaceful between the mossy boles of the old trees. Pink sorrel grew amongst the lush green weeds, making a brilliant carpet. I walked in the dappled shade with Chiang at my heels, waiting for him while he paused to investigate and snuffle something of interest. We came to a glade lit by a bright patch of sunlight. I picked him up and climbed a steep bank fringed with slender saplings and found a shallow grassy hollow; I lay down and drew him into my arms. He was tired and looked at me sleepily, then his eyes glazed and closed. I too became drowsy and we both slept.

I awoke with a start. I heard a light laugh and the murmur of voices, and sat up, cautiously peering through the screen of saplings.

Adonis and Lettie walked hand in hand into the glade. He was wearing his khaki working clothes, the shirt open to the navel. She was dressed in her pink uniform without the apron, and her feet were bare. They stopped in the centre of the glade and faced each other in hushed silence. Her head drooped and she prodded the soft earth with her bare toes.

He smiled, and stretching out his hands started to unbutton the top of her dress. Startled, she stepped back and playfully slapped his hand. His smile broadened, and he moved towards her laying his hands on her breasts. She kept her eyes lowered and he whispered and started to unbutton her dress; then with sudden shocking violence jerked it savagely, half wrenching it off her shoulder and ripping it to the hem. Trina was right – Lettie wore nothing underneath her dress.

She gave a startled cry and stared at him as though mesmerized, making no attempt to hide her body. Without taking her eyes from him she slowly shrugged her shoulders and the dress slid down and fell in pink folds at her feet.

A bright shaft of sunlight spot-lighted her golden-brown body; the full ripe breasts, the softly-rounded belly and the heavy fully-fleshed thighs and buttocks. Her mouth opened and she started to pant. With a single high cry she threw herself into his arms.

I turned away quickly, picked up Chiang, my heart beating too fast and silently crept out of the forest. When I reached the path I clutched him tightly in my arms and ran back to the house.

Chapter Seven

WHEN I WENT down to breakfast on Thursday morning I
found *Ou* Christiaan's two grand-daughters Sannie and
Hettie on their knees, polishing the floors in the hall and
sitting-room in preparation for Trina's dinner-party.
The copper and brass lay stacked on the floor in the
servery. Lettie sat at the table polishing the silver, and
the two tall silver candelabra stood on a table in the
corner. Only Bella was allowed to polish them, which
she always did with an air of importance.

Johan had started his breakfast. 'Ma always makes
such a fuss when she has people to dinner,' he grumbled.
'The way she's carrying on, you'd think Royalty was
coming to dine.' He frowned as Trina entered the room.
She sat at her place with a martyred sigh. 'Ma, why are
you making such a fuss and palaver? Why are you having
the floors, brass and copper polished? Who d'you think
will notice it tonight?'

She poured herself a cup of coffee. 'Bettie would
notice at once if my house wasn't clean.' She helped
herself to sugar. 'I'd see if her house was dirty and her
furniture unpolished. She turned to me. 'Anna, there
won't be time for you to walk with Johannes this morning. We must pick and arrange the flowers.' I looked
down to hide my disappointment.

When Trina and I went into the garden, we met *Ou* Christiaan shuffling towards the kitchen, carrying a big basket of vegetables. When he saw us he lifted his hat. 'Look *Ou Nooi*,' he held the basket towards Trina. 'I pick beautiful young vegetables.' They were artistically arranged in the long basket. Pale baby carrots. A mound of fresh green peas with the dew on them. A snow-white cauliflower and small new potatoes.

'Very nice, very nice,' she said brusquely. 'Now hurry up, Christiaan, there's work to do – don't dawdle in the kitchen!'

She ordered *Ou* Attie to climb the magnolia tree and cut three sprays of flowers. Morose and unsmiling, his black face peered at her through the branches. 'Not that one. Not that one, Attie. Don't be so stupid! Why don't you look where I'm pointing?' She reached up to take the branch and it slipped from her fingers, falling to the ground. 'Now look what you've done! All the petals are knocked off. Why don't you listen when I speak to you?' She turned on me. 'Hurry up Anna! Why are standing about doing nothing? Why haven't you started picking the primroses?' Her brows knitted. 'Where's Christiaan – why isn't he here?' She harried and bullied all of us.

I crouched on my knees picking primroses and violets until my legs and back ached. Trina cut sprays of weigelia and branches of the late pinkish-mauve azalea. She filled her boat-shaped basket with crab-apple blossom and sweet-smelling lilac. 'Now, Anna, pick me two dozen pale pink camellias – the single one with the yellow stamens growing against the south wall. Then we'll have a cup of tea.'

After tea we arranged the flowers. Branches of the pink magnolia bloomed in the tall white metal Batavian cuspidor, which she placed on the slate-topped table in the sitting-room. The primroses stood on the Queen

Anne desk and a bowl of deep purple Parma violets on the sofa table. Sprays of crab-apple and weigelia were arranged in a silver wine-cooler in the hall. Delicate pale pink camellias gleamed in a flat silver bowl on the old stinkwood dining-room table.

Tant' Bettie and *Oom* Gert were the first guests to arrive for dinner. *Tant'* Bettie liked to arrive early so that she could look at Trina's garden. She wore a pale blue lace dress which made her look dowdy. Trina on the other hand appeared slim and elegant in a flamboyant silk dress.

They walked on to the lawn and I saw *Tant'* Bettie glance inquisitively at the herbaceous border. 'I see, not much has been planted out.'

'No,' Trina said shortly. 'I started rather late. How's your border doing?'

'It was finished weeks ago. I've never seen it look better.'

Trina lit a cigarette and blew out the match. 'Bettie, I'm so pleased to hear about Maria's engagement to John Graham.'

'*Ag*, Trina, I'm so happy for her.'

'Tell me, is John by any chance the son of Dr Philip Graham who lives in Somerset West?'

'Yes he is,' *Tant'* Bettie said firmly. She caught *Oom* Gert's sleeve and drew him to her, tucking her hand into the crook of his arm. 'Gert and I know that Philip Graham drinks,' she said clearly, looking Trina straight in the eye. 'And we're both delighted that Maria's going to marry his son – aren't we, Gert?'

'Absolutely delighted!' he boomed, drawing himself up and staring hard at Trina.

For once she was disconcerted with nothing to say

and seemed relieved to see Colonel Jamieson crossing the lawn.

He was a tall distinguished man in his early sixties, with a neatly clipped military moustache and a florid complexion. 'My dear Trina, how charming you look!' He took her hand and kissed it gallantly.

'Dear James, how nice to have you back with us.' She smiled, and took his arm. *Oom* Gert, *Tant'* Bettie and I followed them into the house.

We found Johan talking to Mr and Mrs North. He was a nondescript silent man. His wife on the other hand, was a voluptuous questing woman – her white décolleté dress barely concealing her magnificent bosom. *Oom* Gert's eyes bulged when he saw her.

I joined Johan at the table where an assortment of bottles, decanters and glasses glittered under the light.

He looked me up and down. 'I like your dress.'

I smiled. 'I see you're wearing your courting clothes.'

Mrs North came over to us. 'What are you two talking about?'

'May I offer you a drink, Mrs North?' Johan asked politely.

'Oh please don't call me Mrs North,' she laid her hand on his sleeve. 'Call me Marianna.'

He grinned. 'Will you have a drink, Marianna?'

'A scotch and soda, Johan. With very little soda. D'you know that I am one of your greatest fans?' She was standing very close to him. 'I couldn't believe it when your mother told me your rugby days were over!'

I left them and went to sit next to *Tant'* Bettie. '*Ag*, Anna, I'm so happy that you and Maria are such good friends.' She was watching *Oom* Gert who had joined Johan and Marianna.

Half an hour later Lettie called us in to dinner. As we trooped through the hall I saw *Oom* Gert put his arm around Marianna's waist. His hand slipped down and stroked her hip, then gently pinched her bottom. She squealed and laughingly smacked him. *Tant'* Bettie was next to me and when we reached the dining-room she hastily opened her bag, took out a handkerchief and dabbed her eyes.

Colonel Jamieson was placed next to me and turned to me courteously. 'Trina tells me that you've kindly offered to type my book and help me with my correspondence.'

I smiled shyly. 'Yes, I'd like to do it, but I hope Trina's told you that I'm not very experienced.'

'I'm delighted, my dear,' his smile was genial. 'Perhaps I could come along on Monday morning and have a little chat with you. I'll bring my book and a few letters for you to type.'

'I'm quite sure Trina could arrange for me to come to your place,' I said quickly.

'Not at all, not at all.' He looked to Trina who was sitting at the head of the table, her face glowing in the candle-light. 'I'm always delighted to have an excuse for coming to Wonderkloof to see my dear Trina.' The look Trina gave him verged on being coy.

Johan looked up and caught my eye. His face remained expressionless as he dropped an eyelid.

After dinner we had coffee in the sitting-room and then sat down to bridge. I played with Marianna, Johan and *Oom* Gert. None of us were good, but Marianna's bridge was atrocious and scatterbrained. When she made a mistake *Oom* Gert fondly patted her hand or stroked her arm. It was plain that he could barely restrain himself from patting the soft rosy mounds so invitingly displayed.

Marianna for her part, was having the same difficulty in restraining herself from touching Johan. She'd put

58

her hand on his sleeve, or impulsively grasp his hand. Twice she stretched across the table to pat his bony obstinate chin. I saw his eyes drop speculatively to her bosom. He looked sideways and seeing me staring at him, gave a bland smile.

The guests left at half past eleven. *Oom* Gert and *Tant'* Bettie were the last to leave. As they walked down the steps, he put his arm around her waist, but she pushed him angrily away. When she was seated in the car, she dried her eyes and blew her nose, keeping her face turned from us.

'Poor Bettie,' Trina said as I helped her empty the ashtrays and collect the scorers. 'How I'd hate to have a husband like Gert – ogling and pawing every pretty woman he sees.' She picked up the cards, scorers and pencils, and put them in a drawer of the Queen Anne desk. 'I was fortunate. My Jan never looked at another woman.'

'God help him if he had!' Johan said succinctly. He grinned as he leaned indolently against the mantelpiece, munching a chocolate.

'Johannes! There'll be no blasphemy in this house.' She removed the opulent purple cloth from the bridge table and folded it neatly. 'I found it downright disgusting the way Gert ogled that woman's bosom.'

I took Chiang from Isabella's arms and held him against my face. 'He wasn't the only one,' I murmured.

'What,' she glared at Johan. 'Not you too, Johannes!' He smiled sheepishly. She angrily flicked the cloth from the second bridge table. 'There are times when I've grave fears that you take after your grandfather.'

He tweaked Chiang's ears. 'And have a mistress at Wonderkloof? That's what will happen, Ma, if you succeed in marrying me off to one of those girls you're always inviting to stay here.'

She stood very straight. 'I wouldn't try to pick your wife, Johannes,' she said with dignity. 'I find it difficult to understand that you're always out – yet never bring the girls to your home.' She looked at him when he made no reply. 'I'd have thought you'd be proud of Wonderkloof.' She paused. 'Perhaps,' she added, her voice a little deeper, 'you're ashamed of your old mother.'

'Well, it's well past my bedtime.' He stroked Chiang's head and kissed my cheek. 'Good-night, Anna.' He bent and kissed Trina. 'Good-night, Ma.' Then he put his arm around her and drew her to him, putting his cheek against her face. 'Sleep well.'

Chapter Eight

WE SAT IN the shade of the magnolia tree and watched Lettie approaching with the tea-tray. Trina brushed away the petals and Lettie smiled as she placed the tray carefully in the centre of the table. When she'd gone Trina looked at me and raised her eyebrows. 'What's happened to the child?' she exclaimed. 'She's completely changed – thank goodness! and she and Bella have stopped their incessant quarrelling.'

Lettie's full mouth was usually curved in a soft smile and she hummed monotonously and happily all day. She gaily teased Bella; but her mother remained heavily silent. I often saw Bella look at her daughter with deep suspicion, a puzzled frown on her black face.

Trina poured the tea and handed me the raisin-bread. 'Johannes told me that he won't be gallivanting to-night,' she said, stirring her tea, 'so I thought it would be a good opportunity for him to explain the running of the farm to you. He'll be able to give you an idea of what's required in the way of book-keeping, and the letters to be answered.'

'I'm longing to start.'

That night after dinner, I followed Trina and Johan into his book-lined study. The heavy olive-green curtains were drawn, and Johan switched on the standard lamp behind his desk. 'Running a farm's rather like running a business,' he said, settling himself comfortably in the chair behind his desk. 'Only much harder work,' he added, with a wry smile.

I put Chiang on the chair next to me, and Isabella jumped up with a miaow and started to lick him.

I was horrified by the vast sums of money paid out for agricultural machinery, wages, tools, sprays and fertilizers. Even the money spent on such seemingly small articles like sulphur for the vines, woodwool and wood for the fruit trays made in the packing sheds, bottles for the wine and labels for the fruit boxes, reached frightening proportions. 'The labels on our bottles aren't good,' Johan said, looking at Trina. 'We're producing good wine, but our labels are dull and unimaginative. We'll have to do something about it.' For once she was in agreement with him.

During the eighteen months I worked in Pretoria, I was fortunate to be employed by a middle-aged Jew who owned a small but prosperous business. With infinite kindness and patience he taught me to be systematic. 'Streamline your work and be methodical, Miss van Reenen,' he always said. 'Don't clutter up your mind or your desk, and you'll save us both a lot of trouble.'

It was easy to see that neither Trina nor Johan were streamlined or methodical.

I glanced at Johan and cleared my throat nervously. 'Johan.'

He looked at me enquiringly. 'Yes?'

'Won't you let me arrange your desk in a more businesslike way?'

His brows drew together and he bristled as though I'd insulted him. 'Nobody may touch anything on my desk,' he said curtly. 'I don't even like it dusted if it means that my papers will be messed about.'

'Please, Johan!' I pleaded. 'I promise I won't mess up anything. I'll file and mark everything so that you'll know where your papers are kept.' He remained uncompromisingly silent. I smiled and pointed at his desk. 'Look at your desk – it's all cluttered up!'

He didn't return my smile. 'It's not cluttered up. I know exactly where everything is.'

'Johan,' I persisted. 'I'll arrange it so that you'll be able to put out your hand in the dark and find what you want.'

He looked at me darkly. 'You're getting like Ma,' he growled.

I spent the next day clearing out his desk and setting it in order. Everything was dusted and carefully filed. I was dusty, tired but happy – confident I'd done the job well.

After dinner I waited impatiently for Johan to finish his coffee. As soon as he put down his cup, I jumped up gathering Chiang in my arms. 'Come, Johan, I want to show you what I've done. Come, Trina!'

He stood up with obvious reluctance and slowly followed us into his study. He crossed to his desk, and looked at it. 'Where are my papers?' he suddenly asked, looking at me angrily. 'What are these two damned trays doing on my desk?' He flipped one contemptuously.

My heart started to beat quickly. 'The tray on the right contains the letters to be answered – and the accounts to be paid,' I said timidly, trying to keep the quaver out of my voice. 'When you've checked them, put them in the other tray, and I'll type the letters and see that they're posted.'

'Humph,' he grunted. He was now standing behind the desk frowning slightly and ruffling through the papers in the tray.

'I've typed cards and put them in the slots in front of each drawer,' I said quickly. I joined him behind the desk. 'If you look here you'll see—'

'Yes. Yes. I can see,' he interrupted impatiently. He was still frowning. He pulled a drawer open, looked into it and shut it again without comment.

'You've done it beautifully, Anna!' Trina said, joining us behind the desk. 'It's so businesslike, darling. It simplifies everything,' she looked at Johan. 'Hasn't she done it well, Johannes?' she asked brightly.

'Humph,' he grunted without looking up.

Not a word of praise. Not a word of thanks. My eyes filled with tears. I picked up Chiang and walked out of the room. On the way to my bedroom, he snuffled and licked my cheek in sympathy.

Later that night, Trina tapped on my door. I was typing the first chapter of Colonel Jamieson's book. 'Good-night, darling. Don't work too late.' She ran her hand through my hair. 'What silky hair you have.' When I looked up she smiled. 'Don't take any notice of Johannes, darling. He's being typically masculine. You've done a wonderful job and he knows it!'

The fluted edges of the swimming-pool were newly white-washed and the clear water glinted brightly blue in the brilliant sunshine.

On Sunday afternoon, Trina was reading near the pool under the white-barked paper birch. Maria and John lay sunbathing on the lawn, and I sat under the beach umbrella with Chiang on my lap.

Trina's roses were in full bloom. In the formal rose-garden each segment cut out of the lawn was a different colour. Climbers cloaked the garden walls with golden red and pink blooms. The ramblers spilled over the walls to hang in heavy scented clusters.

64

Maria gave a soft exclamation and lifted her eyebrows. 'Look who's arrived!' she said in a stage whisper. 'You'll never guess! Johan and his girl-friend and the Black Prince with his latest blonde.' She always called Julian 'the Black Prince'. It suited his dark good looks and faintly haughty air.

They stopped and talked to Trina and then crossed the lawn and disappeared through the second door in the high wall which hid the two changing rooms. Julian was the first to reappear. He greeted us coolly and when the blonde came through the doorway, took her arm and formally introduced us. Still holding her, he led her to the other side of the pool where they sat in isolation for the rest of the afternoon.

Johan's lean athletic body towered over his diminutive girl-friend. 'Anna, I don't think you and Molly have met.'

'Hi, Anna,' she smiled vivaciously. She saw Chiang and scooped him out of my lap. 'Oh, my darling Chiang, how you've grown! You darling itsy witsy angel.' She buried her face in his fur. 'Don't you absolutely adore him?' she asked me, kissing the top of his head.

'Yes, I love him very much,' I blushed and felt awkward.

She walked over to Trina cradling Chiang in her arms. 'Oh, Mrs de Villiers, isn't Chiang simply adorable? Though he was the smallest of the litter Mummy always said he'd be a beauty. And you *are* a beauty!' She held him up and kissed him again.

Trina turned her book face down on her lap and looked at her over the top of her spectacles. 'Does your mother breed pekinese?' she asked affably.

'Yes, we've three gorgeous bitches with pedigrees a mile long, and last year Mummy imported a divine and madly expensive dog.' She turned and surveyed the garden. 'What an absolutely fantastic garden! – I've never seen anything like it. And the roses! There must be thousands – how many trees have you got?'

'About five hundred,' Trina said pleasantly.

'Five hundred – five hundred rose trees! Hannie!' she called to Johan. 'You're very naughty! You never told me about your mother's wonderful garden.'

He was sitting on the edge of the pool, nibbling a blade of grass and glanced up briefly then looked back into the translucent depths of the pool. He was silent and absent all afternoon.

She, on the other hand, never stopped talking and Trina seemed to encourage her incessant babbling.

At five o'clock Johan looked at his watch. 'We must be going.'

'Why don't you stay and have supper?' Trina asked hospitably.

Molly clapped her hands. 'Oh, I'd adore that! I'd simply love it.'

'I'm sorry,' Johan said abruptly. 'I've a hard day tomorrow. I'll take you home now.'

'Oh, Hannie!' she wailed. 'I think you're mean!' she pouted charmingly. 'Don't you think he's a nasty meanie, Mrs de Villiers?'

At breakfast the following morning Trina was fidgety and repeatedly looked at Johan while he ate his porridge. 'Johannes,' she said at last.

He looked up warily. 'Yes, Ma?'

'That girl – does she always talk so much?'

'No.'

'She never stopped talking the whole afternoon.' He continued eating his porridge and she buttered her toast. 'That name she calls you, Johannes. Is it an abbreviation or is she calling you Honey?'

'I've no idea, I've never asked her.'

She carefully cut the toast into thin fingers. 'Johannes, you're not going to marry that girl?'

'No, Ma.'

My heart leapt.

'Not marry her!' Her voice was scandalized. 'I believe you've been going out with the poor child for a year.' She stared at him when he made no reply. 'Did you ever intend marrying her?'

He looked up, his face hard. 'Ma, will you stop trying to run my life!'

She drew the tray nearer and lifted the coffee-pot. 'I'm so glad you're not going to – she'd have driven us both mad.' His chair scraped as he pushed it back. 'You haven't finished your breakfast, Johannes! Aren't you going to drink your coffee?'

He looked at me, his face taut with anger. 'Are you coming?'

I quickly followed him out of the room. That morning we walked in silence.

Chapter Nine

'TRINA,' I SAID. 'I'm wondering if Bella could pack a picnic basket. I'm taking Martin up to the *Kloof* on Sunday.'

She looked at me over the top of her spectacles. 'I don't like your going alone with him.'

'Why not?' I asked, feeling a spark of rebellion.

She removed her spectacles and placed them carefully on the table. 'Because it isn't safe. Anything could happen.'

'What could happen, Ma?' Johan asked, lifting his eyebrows.

'Johannes,' she said sharply. 'Will you kindly not interfere!' She turned back to me. 'It's lonely up there, and the cliffs are dangerous.'

'You never worried about the cliffs being dangerous when you wanted Julian and me to plant your disas.'

'Johannes, I'm speaking to Anna – not to you!'

'In any case,' I said placatingly. 'We won't be alone. John and Maria are going with us.'

'Oh.' There was a long pause. 'Ask them to have dinner here in the evening. I'll get Bella to bake a chicken pie.'

The walk to the *Kloof* was no longer the wearying *trek* it had been seven years ago when I saw it for the first time. Now the vineyards encroached more and more on the mountain slopes. Each year fresh ground was cleared and new vines planted. To reach them, Johan had made a rough contour drive.

We borrowed his jeep and left it at the side of the road about one and a half miles from the *Kloof* in the shade of an old laurel pushing its way through an outcrop of granite boulders. We took the narrow stony footpath leading up to the grove of trees we could see in the distance and ate our lunch next to the stream in the deep shade of the trees. Martin sat opposite me leaning against a rock, his feet in the water and his dark damp hair clinging to his forehead in little tendrils.

I went and stood on the edge of the cliff and looked cautiously over the edge. 'Look!' I cried. 'The *waboom*'s still alive, but the leaves are turning yellow – it's going to die. Next year Johan will be able to chop it out.'

After lunch we clambered down the path and stood in the glade at the edge of the dark pool, looking at the dripping crag, bejewelled with hundreds of disas.

'Isn't it wonderful!' I cried.

'It's fantastic!' Martin said with awe.

Maria was sitting on the grass bank. 'Anna, d'you know that *Tant'* Trina's responsible for planting most of the disas in the *Kloof*?'

'Is she?'

'People from all over the Western Province sent her disas. They arrived in their hundreds! Every weekend we trudged up here with our knapsacks stuffed with them. There was hardly room for our food. *Tant'* Trina always walked behind shouting at us to hurry up. Johan, Julian and their friends climbed the cliffs and planted them while she stood at the edge of the pool, shouting instructions.' She laughed. 'Johan always said, "Ma wouldn't care if we broke our damned necks as long as the disas were planted where she wanted them".'

When we returned to the house John and Martin had a swim and I took Maria to my room. She sat in front of the dressing-table powdering her nose and I on the edge of my bed, cradling Chiang in my arms.

I saw her looking at me in the mirror. 'Anna, you know that Martin's in love with you?'

'Nonsense!' my cheeks were warm. 'Just because—'

'Of course he is,' she interrupted. 'It sticks out a mile.' She turned and faced me. 'D'you love him?'

I moved uncomfortably and avoided looking at her. 'No, I like him very much but I'm not in love with him.'

She looked at herself in the mirror and ran my comb through her smooth fair hair. 'It's someone else, isn't it?'

I jumped up and walked to the window. 'No,' I said firmly. 'There's no one else.' Only Chiang was allowed to share my secret.

'Tell me,' Trina said to Martin during dinner. 'Is your father Martin Joubert, the attorney at Tulbagh?'

'Yes, Mrs de Villiers.'

'Ah! I used to know him when I was a girl.' She glanced up and smiled. 'You're very like him.' She held her glass to the light. 'Look at the candle-light shining through the wine – it glows like a ruby. This is our Wonderkloof Cabernet. D'you like it?'

'It's excellent.'

'Are you following in the family footsteps and taking law?'

'Yes.'

'I suppose you'll join the firm?'

'Yes, when I've taken my degree I'll join my father.'

She nodded and smiled. 'How pleased he must be. You'll be the fourth generation?'

70

'Yes.'

When it was time to leave I walked with him to the car. We waved goodbye to Maria and John and then he turned to me. 'Good-night, Anna. Thank you for a wonderful day.' There was no moon and his face was a white blur in the dark. He took my arms, drawing me to him, and kissed me on the mouth. 'Good-night, darling,' he whispered. His kiss was soft and warm.

We'd nearly finished breakfast. Trina poured the coffee. 'This boy, Anna. This Martin Joubert you're seeing so often. I knew his father when I was a girl.'

'So you told us last night.'

She passed me the sugar. 'His father was an intelligent, attractive man. Good-looking and extremely able.' I looked at her silently. 'But he was the biggest *skelm* in Tulbagh – like his father before him.'

'I don't care!' I cried, my cheeks burning. 'I don't care if Martin's father and grandfather were the two biggest *skelms* in South Africa. He's sweet and kind and I like him!'

'His father was also sweet and kind.' I pushed my cup away and sprang to my feet. 'Finish your coffee, Anna!'

'I don't want any.' I looked at Johan impatiently. 'Are you coming, Johan!'

He looked up, trying to hide a smile. 'Yes.' He followed me, picked up his hat from the *rusbank* and we walked down the steps together. 'You like him very much, don't you?'

'Yes, I do.' I picked up Chiang and held him against my face. 'But I don't love him, if that's what you're insinuating.'

'I'm not insinuating anything.'

'I like him,' I said aggressively, 'and don't give a damn if his father and grandfather were *skelms*!'

71

'Good Lord, I've never heard you swear before.'

'You taught me!' I said tartly. I looked up and saw Adonis waiting for him. 'I must go to Trina.'

He smiled. 'I'm glad you're living with us. You're good for Ma.' He paused, and lightly touched my cheek. 'You're restful – like your mother – and you have her eyes.'

I looked at him speechlessly, then quickly turned and ran back to the house. 'Oh, Chiang,' I whispered clasping him tightly. 'I'm so happy.'

Trina was in the kitchen talking to Bella. 'Bella has just been telling me that she's taking Lettie to Paarl next Sunday afternoon to meet a young man, who's a carpenter.'

Bella drew herself to her full majestic height and folded her arms. 'His parents is respectable godfearing people, Miss Anna. I know his mother for a long time. She want her son to marry a decent hardworking girl. She say the girls where they live is a no good, rubbishy lot.' Lettie was washing up the breakfast dishes and Bella looked at her fondly. 'My Lettie's a decent girl. She go to Church every Sunday, and sleep in the room with her mother. She don't run around at night in the bushes like other girls.' Lettie glanced at Bella and preened herself. 'He live with his mother and father, *Merrem*,' Bella said to Trina. 'He and his father have a big business. They make furniture for all the rich white people of Paarl.' Bella was the only coloured person at Wonderkloof who called Trina 'Madam'. To the rest of the *volk* she was known as '*Ou Nooi*'. 'Lettie, my little love,' she cried. 'You have a bath on Sunday morning and put on your best pink satin dress.'

'Yes, Mammie.'

That afternoon I looked out of my bedroom window and saw Lettie returning from the oak forest. She was walking sedately down the shady path. Suddenly she smiled to herself, kicked up her heels and skipped along like a little girl.

The next morning I found a letter lying on my side-plate. Picking it up with reluctance I read it and then sat back in silence.

Trina looked at me. 'What's the matter, Anna? Who's the letter from?'

'Uncle Charles,' I muttered. 'Read it,' I pushed it over to her. 'He wants me to stay with them and has offered to pay my fare.'

She put on her spectacles, opened the letter and scanned it quickly. 'I think you should go, they're your only relatives. You'll like Charles. He's very like your mother and Elizabeth is a good woman.'

Leave Wonderkloof. Leave Johan. Leave Chiang. Travel alone! 'I don't want to go!' I cried childishly.

She smiled. 'I'll go with you, I haven't been to Europe for four years and I've a hankering to see it again. We'll leave at the end of April.' I stared out of the window. 'You haven't travelled before, and should see something of the world. I'd like to show you the Matterhorn but I think we'll have to leave that for next time. Now you should spend a month with Charles and Elizabeth and get to know them. They've no children and I can see that they're anxious to meet you.' I looked at my plate without speaking. 'I know that you and your Uncle will get on. Next week when we go to Cape Town I'll see about our booking.'

'Ma's a great organizer,' Johan said with a grin.

I looked at him sourly.

Chapter Ten

IT WAS THE beginning of summer. The first flush of roses was over in Trina's garden, and the hydrangeas under the remaining old pear tree were deep blue. St Joseph and Regale lilies grew in clumps next to the paths and bloomed in the cuspidor on the table in the sitting-room.

The early peaches were ripening and arriving in lorry loads at the packing-sheds to be graded and packed by the coloured women from the cottages. Trina and Bella were at the sheds all day, packing and supervising.

Trina refused to allow me to assist them. 'Darling, you're doing a much more useful job than packing fruit: even Johannes admits we're more businesslike. You get on with James' book, our accounts and letters, and Bella and I will get on with the packing.'

Maria invited me to spend the day. Before leaving I went to say goodbye to Trina.

'Have a look at Bettie's herbaceous border while you're there.' She was wrapping the graded peaches and packing them into trays lined with woodwool.

'I'll have a look at her border,' I said, 'but I'm not very knowledgeable about plants.'

'You know what delphiniums, salpiglossis, dahlias, phlox and petunias look like,' she said, holding a peach

74

and looking impatient. 'Just make a note of what's growing in the beds.'

Tant' Bettie's border was further advanced than Trina's and the plants were better grown. There were clumps of healthy perennial phlox, and between them, patches of lush salpiglossis twice the size of Trina's.

'Impossible!' she cried when I told her this the next morning.

'I'm almost sure they're salpiglossis,' I said. 'They're exactly the same as yours, only twice as big.'

'Stop harping on their size!' she said irritably.

It was Sunday morning, and Colonel Jamieson was having tea with us in the garden. She jumped up and crossed the lawn to stand in front of the long curved bed with her hands on her hips, surveying it despondently. 'It's not good this year,' she shook her head. 'The plants aren't thriving. I think I've planted everything too late.' She came back and sat down, feeling in the pocket of her gardening smock for her cigarette case. 'I'm devoted to Bettie. No one knows better than I what a good friend she is – but she tends to be smug.' She wrung her hands. 'She'll be unbearable!'

Colonel Jamieson got up, struck a match and lit her cigarette. 'My dearest Trina, don't allow yourself to get so upset. D'you remember how much you and Bettie admired the dahlias I imported from Holland last year? My dear, they're yours if you'd care to have them, and you may also have the tall blue penstemon which I managed to smuggle through the customs.'

'Oh, James, you're so kind!' She touched his hand. 'Anna,' she smiled. 'Will you fetch them tomorrow afternoon?'

The next day in the cool of the evening, *Ou* Attie and *Ou* Christiaan worked overtime and Trina's border was rearranged.

On Tuesday night she dined with Colonel Jamieson. She came into the sitting-room wearing a long cyclamen skirt and an elegant black blouse. Johan jumped up and gave a long low whistle. 'You'll knock him sideways, Ma.'

She smiled and looked at her watch. 'He should be here soon. It's sure to be one of those dreary social evenings. I'm devoted to James,' she dropped her voice and looked over her shoulder, 'but he's a dreadful snob. Haven't you noticed, Anna, what a name-dropper he is in those dull books he writes?'

A moment later he came into the sitting-room, smiling and debonair. 'My dearest Trina. You look quite charming!' He took her hands and held her away so that he could look at her.

She kissed us good-night and took Colonel Jamieson's arm. When they reached the door she turned and smiled archly. 'Don't get into mischief, you two!'

'What mischief, Ma?' Johan said dryly.

After dinner, we sat in his study going through the accounts.

'Johan, d'you think that Trina will marry Colonel Jamieson?'

'Are you mad!' he exclaimed, his eyebrows raised in astonishment.

'It's not such a silly question,' I said a trifle huffily. 'He's attractive and it's obvious they're fond of each other.'

'My dear Anna,' he smiled. 'Ma's had men interested in her ever since Pa died. She's not only a wealthy widow. She's also intelligent and feminine. She could have remarried a dozen times.' He sat back. 'I remember some years ago she saw that I was worried that she might marry one of her more persistent admirers. She came in here and stood in front of my desk and said,

'Johannes, I'm a one man woman". Then raised her chin, "And Jan was my man," she added.' He grinned. 'Mind you, I wouldn't put it past Ma to have an occasional flutter.'

'Really, Johan! What d'you mean by an occasional flutter?'

'Come,' he said with an amused smile. 'You know what I mean. I don't think Ma would look half as good if she didn't have a man to warm her up occasionally.'

I looked down my nose and remained silent.

That night we witnessed the beginning of a friendship between Chiang and Wolf.

Chiang jumped off the chair, went to Wolf, sniffed his face and licked him. Wolf opened his eyes, then pushed his nose under Chiang's belly and tipped him over so that he fell on his back. His eyes bulged with astonishment and he leapt to his feet, wagging his tail and barking shrilly – Wolf tumbled and rolled over and in a flash Chiang sprang at his throat.

We forgot our work and for nearly quarter of an hour sat in silence watching them playing. I still remember the singularly tender expression on Johan's face.

When we'd finished I stood up, yawned and stretched. 'Well, I'm off to bed.'

He glanced at his watch and got up. 'Yes, it's well past my bedtime.'

We reached the door at the same time. 'Good-night,' I said self-consciously.

'Good-night.'

This time he didn't kiss my cheek but drew me swiftly and surely into his arms and kissed me on the mouth – it was quite unlike Martin's soft kisses and my heart lurched and started to beat quickly. He felt my response, tightened his arms and the kiss deepened.

Then he looked down at me, his long grey eyes shining

into mine. 'This must be the mischief Ma was talking about.' He tilted my chin, smiled and kissed me gently, 'You're sweet. Go on, you'd better go to bed.'

The next week Trina left Bella in charge of the packing-sheds and we drove to Cape Town early in the morning to do our Christmas shopping.

'Bella asked me to buy her eight yards of white satin for Lettie's wedding-dress. Apparently the young man and his parents approved of her. Bella had them all to tea last Sunday afternoon, while you were gallivanting with that Joubert boy.' She took her eye off the road to glance at me. 'I found them respectable decent people. The prospective bridegroom is a polite, well-spoken young man – far too good for Lettie.'

'When are they getting married?'

'It will have to be in April, just before we leave. I told Bella that I'll give Lettie a slap-up wedding, but we'll be too busy to have it before then – what with packing fruit and harvesting grapes. In any case, Bella will be very busy. She's making Lettie's wedding-dress and also the dresses for the two bridesmaids. She makes clothes for most of the coloured women on the farm. Last night I found Annekie in the kitchen, fitting on the dress Bella's making her for Christmas. The poor child had a nasty gash on her throat and when I asked her what had happened, she looked at the floor and wouldn't answer me. Bella told me later that Adonis was drunk again on Friday night and threatened to cut Annekie's throat – two of the *volk* had to drag him off her.'

'I hate him!' I cried. 'He's a vicious animal. Why doesn't Johan get rid of him?'

She looked at me in surprise. 'I agree with Johannes that Adonis is a good foreman and we're lucky to have him. He controls the *volk* and he's hardworking and reliable. Did you know that he watched every match Johannes played in the Cape? One year I arranged a lift for him to Johannesburg so that he could watch him play in the third Test against the All Blacks. He worships Johannes and will do anything for him.'

'He's horrible! It's not only his brutality – it's also the way he preys on the young girls.'

'Johannes always says, if it wasn't Adonis, it would be someone else.'

'I don't understand Johan, or the *volk* for that matter, they're all friendly with him and don't seem to mind him seducing their daughters and giving them extra mouths to feed.'

'The women do. They're all against him. Except the young ones, of course,' she added with a sardonic smile.

Trina kept a list of every coloured man, woman and child at Wonderkloof. At the wholesale store she bought toys and sweets for the children, rattles for the babies, dress lengths for the women, shirts and tobacco for the men. While I did my Christmas shopping, she went to the travel agency and made our booking.

At half past twelve we drove through the school gates and found Pieter waiting for us. He smiled happily, and kissed us. 'Gee, Ma. You're late!'

'I'm sorry, darling. We had so much to do. How did the exams go?'

'All right, I think I've passed.'

Chapter Eleven

WHENEVER I THINK of Wonderkloof in December that year, I remember the hot days and the riot of colour in Trina's garden. The hibiscus and Pride of India were in flower and the pale shell-pink Bougainvillea Natalia covered the summer-house. Trina's herbaceous border was at its best for Christmas.

'Ag, Trina,' *Tant'* Bettie said sadly. 'Your border is beautiful! I've never seen it look better. Mine's so disappointing – the salpiglossis are over, and the petunias are already shabby. I put my plants in too early.'

During those hot days it was always cool and peaceful in the old house. I remember the fruit on the side-board underneath the portrait of Johan's great-grandmother, Gertrude Barton. Bowls of golden pink-cheeked apricots, fat rosy peaches and purple plums with the bloom on them. Sometimes there was a bowl of late strawberries, small, sweet and red.

I think of Bella in the kitchen making the Christmas pudding, fruit cake and mince pies. And Lettie sitting at the kitchen table, laughing and talking to her while she stoned the raisins and chopped up the citroen peel and green fig preserve.

That year the Christmas lunch was at Wonderkloof and *Tant'* Bettie, *Oom* Gert, Julian and Maria sat with us. Trina at the head of the table in a sleeveless shocking-pink linen dress, with Colonel Jamieson on her right and *Oom* Gert on her left.

Trina and Johan carved the steaming roast turkey, the great golden-brown goose and the suckling-pig with a potato in its mouth. Sannie and Hettie helped Lettie hand around the dishes of Christiaan's young vegetables, the sweet potatoes and yellow rice. The curtains were drawn when Bella sailed into the dining-room with the flaming Christmas pudding. Surfeited, we sat around the table drinking our coffee, unable to resist nibbling Bella's *naartjie* preserve and pecking disinterestedly at the nuts and raisins.

I remember the *volk* standing in the shade of the oaks in front of the house. Annekie wearing the new dress Bella had made her, cradling her baby and staring dully at the ground, with Adonis next to her, smiling confidently. *Ou* Attie and *Ou* Christiaan grizzle-haired and unrecognizable in their dark suits. Lettie, standing demurely next to Bella's vast figure, wearing a bright blue satin dress, the close-fitting glossy material revealing every curve of her luscious ripe body.

I remember the balmy evening I sat on the swing seat in the garden and looking up saw Johan come across the lawn.

'To quote Trina,' I teased, trying to keep my voice natural 'I'm surprised you're not gallivanting tonight.'

'It's too hot for gallivanting.'

He sank down next to me, leant back and took my hand. We sat in silence, then he turned his head and looked at me. 'You're so quiet and serene,' he murmured. He drew me to him so that I lay in his arms looking up at him and put his hand on my breast. 'Not so serene after all,' he whispered. 'I can feel your heart fluttering like a wild bird.'

81

I reached up and pulled his face down to mine.

Trina and I were taken with great ceremony to Bella's bedroom to see Lettie's wedding-dress. 'What, Bella!' Trina exclaimed. 'Don't tell me you've finished. I can't believe it!'

'Yes, *Merrem*,' Bella looked pleased and rather self-satisfied. 'I been working on Lettie's dress day and night. It fit her like a dream. Don't it, my love?' She patted Lettie's cheek and gently pinched her chin. 'Look at the beautiful lace, *Merrem*,' she held the dress out in front of Trina. 'Jes look at all the little tucks and bows what I make. My Lettie's got a wedding-dress fit for a queen!'

'It's beautiful, Bella,' Trina leant forward closely inspecting the fine needlework, then glanced at Lettie and said rather sharply; 'you're a very lucky girl.'

'Yes, I know I lucky, *Ou Nooi*.' She smiled and dropped her eyes.

Bella cleared her throat. 'Now I can relax, *Merrem*. The wedding-dress is finished and the bridesmaids' dresses won't take long.' There was a pregnant pause. 'Then – I make my dress.'

'What will you wear, Bella?'

She bent and took a bolt of purple satin from the bottom drawer of her dressing-table and held it up. 'This what I wear, *Merrem*,' she said proudly, 'and I make a turban to match.'

'Oh, Bella, you'll look truly magnificent!' Trina cried with feeling.

When we walked into the sitting-room she turned to me and said softly, 'I can't take to that child. First she was sulky and insolent – now butter won't melt in her mouth. She's too good to be true – I won't be sorry to see the last of her.'

During dinner that evening she said abruptly, 'Oh, by the way, Johannes.'

He looked up. 'Yes, Ma?'

She paused while Lettie handed him the peas. 'Gert telephoned this evening and asked me to give you a message. He said you must tell Adonis that if he sets foot on Mooi Vlei again he'll have his backside peppered with buckshot.'

Johan grinned. 'What's he been up to?'

'You can guess! Apparently Bettie found him skulking in their backyard with his arm around Ellie. She's their little housemaid,' she said to me. 'I doubt if she's fifteen. Two years ago Adonis got her sister into trouble when she was the same age. Gert says Bettie is so upset that she's been in floods of tears.' Johan looked down and fiddled with his fork. 'You must speak to him, Johannes. It's becoming too much of a good thing.'

He nodded, 'I'll speak to him again. He'll swear he hasn't been near her – and next week he'll seduce her. You know that as well as I do Ma.'

I casually glanced at Lettie. Her flat-planed face was impassive. As the weeks passed a subtle change took place in her. There was a hint of sulkiness and a certain petulance, never shown to Bella, but with me she was often offhand and familiar. This changed and she became silent and brooding.

One morning I found her in my bedroom, leaning against the cupboard, her face clay-coloured and wet with sweat.

'What's wrong, Lettie?' I cried in alarm, 'Are you sick?'

She looked at me breathing quickly. 'Yes, I sick,' she said in a low voice.

'Have you told Bella?'

Her eyes widened with fear. 'What for I tell

Mammie?' Her voice rose. 'It my business I sick.' She looked at me with angry insolence. 'What for you want to tell her I sick?' she cried shrilly.

'I don't intend to tell her,' I said in a bored voice. 'As you so rightly said, it isn't my business.'

Chapter Twelve

BY THE BEGINNING of March I'd finished typing Colonel Jamieson's book; after he'd checked it for corrections, I posted it with a covering letter to his publishers.

'I'm delighted by the way you've done it, my dear Anna,' he said warmly. 'There's hardly a mistake. You're an extremely capable and methodical young woman. My dearest Trina tells me that we'll be seeing one another in London in May.'

'Oh!' I looked at her in surprise. 'You didn't tell me.'

'Didn't I?' she murmured vaguely.

'D'you realize,' I said to Maria the next day, 'that we leave in under five weeks.' I ran my fingers through my hair. 'And I don't want to go,' I added pettishly.

She smiled. 'They say absence makes the heart grow fonder.' I looked at my nails critically. 'Did you know that Johan's no longer taking Molly out?'

'No,' I said indifferently. 'I wonder if they've quarrelled.'

'I've no idea. Julian will be back soon. He's been in Johannesburg for over a fortnight. Johan will be pleased to have him back: they've always hunted in pairs.'

'Um – m,' I mumbled.

'Have you and Johan been invited to the Norths' dance next Friday night?'

'Yes.'

'I suppose Martin's fetching you?'

'Yes, he said he'd pick me up at eight.'

After dinner we were having coffee in the sitting-room when Maria and John burst into the room. 'You'll never guess what's happened!' Maria cried, her eyes sparkling with excitement.

'You and John have broken your engagement,' Johan interrupted.

'Oh, Johan, you're the bottom!' she giggled, and kissed Trina. '*Tant* Trina, Julian's engaged!'

'What!' Johan exclaimed, his expression outraged. 'Julian engaged!'

'Yes,' she smiled, gratified by his reaction. 'Julian 'phoned this evening. His fiancée is flying down with him on Thursday morning.'

'Who is she?' Trina asked.

'Her name's Sarah Lampton, *Tant* Trina, and she lives in Johannesburg.'

'Lampton,' Trina said thoughtfully. 'She must be the daughter of Robert Lampton.' She turned to me. 'You know Lampton's, Anna, the big store in Johannesburg? Her parents must be very wealthy. Julian's done well for himself.

'Julian engaged!' Johan exclaimed again. 'I can't believe it!'

'What's so unbelievable about it?' Trina said impatiently. 'It's high time he settled down. It's time you both did!'

'Don't start on that again, Ma.'

'You'll see Sarah at the Norths' dance on Friday night,' Maria interrupted quickly. 'You've both been invited, haven't you?' She glanced at Johan and me.

I nodded.

He looked at me and smiled, 'Shall we go together, or is Martin fetching you?'

I blushed. 'No, he isn't fetching me.' I avoided Maria's eyes.

'When do they plan to marry?' Trina asked, lighting a cigarette.

'I don't know, *Tant'* Trina – fairly soon, I believe.'

'Julian engaged!' Johan exclaimed for the third time. Like Trina, I felt a sudden spark of irritation.

For some time Bella had been trying to get Trina to finalize the plans for Lettie's wedding. Trina was unco-operative and disorganized and I could see that this puzzled and worried Bella.

The next morning as we were leaving the kitchen, Bella drew herself to her full height. 'Excuse me, *Merrem*,' she said firmly. 'I want to remind you again about the wedding-cake what you promised my Lettie – is it ordered?'

'Oh,' Trina said vaguely, 'the wedding-cake? There's no hurry, I'll see about it sometime this week.' She moved towards the door.

'And the wedding invitations, *Merrem*,' Bella persisted doggedly. 'You said you'd have them printed. Is they done?'

'Oh dear,' Trina twittered. 'Anna, do remind me to 'phone today.'

Bella's full lips were pursed in disapproval and her voice rose. 'The wedding's in four weeks, *Merrem*. I'd like to send the invitations out by the beginning of next week.'

'I'll do it this morning, Bella, I promise. It won't take more than a couple of days to have them done.' She looked at me with a slight frown. 'Come, Anna,' she said impatiently.

'And the reception, *Merrem*,' Bella said loudly, her eyes fixed angrily on Trina. 'Where've you decided to have it?'

'Stop fussing! I've told you before that I'll arrange everything when the time comes.'

She looked over her shoulder as *Ou* Christiaan shuffled into the kitchen carrying his basket of vegetables. He smiled when he saw us and quickly took off his hat, holding out the basket for her inspection. 'Look, *Ou Nooi*. Two sweet melons, nice young beans and gooseberries for *Ou Nooi*.'

She looked critically at the contents of the basket. 'How many times have I told you that I like young carrots! Why d'you persist in pulling them when they're too big?'

His face fell. 'I sorry, *Ou Nooi*.'

'Lettie – take off your apron!' Bella's accusing voice rang through the kitchen.

Startled, I swung around and stared at her. She was glaring at Lettie who was washing up at the sink. At the sound of her mother's voice, Lettie twisted around and faced her, instinctively clutching her apron.

Bella slowly advanced. 'Take if off! Did you hear what I says. Take it off!'

'No,' Lettie whispered, cringing against the sink and clutching her apron with both hands. 'No Mammie. Please!'

Bella caught her arm and jerked her closer. Roughly twisting her around, she undid the apron which slid to the floor. Lettie's dress was undone over her distended stomach and tightly strained across her swollen breasts.

Bella sucked in her breath with a sibilant hiss. 'Who done it?' she whispered, her nostrils flaring.

Lettie cowered away, her mouth wet and flaccid and her eyes wide with terror. 'Please, Mammie!'

'Who done it? Who done it I says!' Bella shouted and struck her a blow across the face.

Lettie screamed and reeled backwards, crashing against the kitchen table.

'Bella! Stop that at once – control yourself!' Trina cried sharply.

Bella in her blind fury didn't hear her. She advanced on Lettie again. 'Who done it?' she shouted. 'Was it Adonis, you dirty slut?'

Lettie screamed. Her head snapped back and her cap fell off at the next blow.

'Answer me! Was it Adonis, you dirty whore?' Bella slammed her clenched fist into Lettie's face and the blood spurted in a bright stream from her nose.

The sight of the blood dripping on to her dress unhinged her completely. 'Yes!' Her ear-splitting shriek was appalling. 'Yes! It was Adonis! It was Adonis! It was Adonis!' It sounded like a needle sticking on a gramophone record. 'It was Adonis!' she screamed. 'Adonis! Adonis!' She turned and ran clumsily out of the kitchen and I heard her stumbling and falling as she ran up the stairs. 'It was Adonis! Adonis!'

Bella slowly crossed the kitchen and sank heavily on to a chair; with a broken cry she covered her face and burst into tears, rocking backwards and forwards in anguish. 'Oh, *Merrem, Merrem!*'

Trina patted her shoulder, hovering over her like a bird. 'There there, Bella.'

'Oh. *Merrem.*' Bella looked up, her mouth trembling and the tears streaming down her cheeks. 'Oh, the shame! The shame! That my own daughter what I bring up to be respectable put this shame on her poor old mother what treat her so good. How can I hold up my head, *Merrem*? What do I tell the bridegroom and his parents? What do I tell my friends?' She wiped her eyes

89

with the corner of her apron. 'And all the money and time what I spend on the wedding-dress and the brides-maids' dresses. What do I say, *Merrem*? Oh, the shame! The shame!'

Trina patted her shoulder again. 'Don't cry, Bella,' she said kindly. 'Your friends will understand. They'll stand by and help you.' A sound made her look across the room and her brows knitted in anger. 'Christiaan!' she exclaimed. 'What are you doing here! Why aren't you working in the garden?' Grimacing in excitement, he was clasping his hat to his chest. 'Go back to the garden at once!'

He bobbed his head and scuttled out of the kitchen like a beetle to spread the news amongst the *volk*.

'I'm surprised,' Trina said later, 'that Bella didn't discover long ago that Lettie was pregnant.'

'I couldn't see anything. When did you notice it for the first time?'

'Weeks ago.'

'How could you tell?'

She smiled and patted my arm. 'I've an experienced eye, my child. We've had pregnant housemaids at Wonderkloof ever since I've lived here.'

'Is that why you didn't order the cake and wedding invitations?'

She nodded. 'Yes. I hoped Bella would notice in time. I don't believe in throwing money away.'

During the following weeks Lettie's mouth was sulky and her face heavily sullen. She never smiled and her manner was insolent. She and Bella quarrelled from morning to night. All day we heard their strident voices raised in the kitchen. Bella no longer referred to her daughter as 'my little love'. Now it was 'you dirty slut', 'you low-class street girl' and 'you whore what bring shame on your poor old mother'.

Chapter Thirteen

'I WONDER WHAT Julian's fiancée will be like?'

It was Friday evening and Johan and I were on our way to the North's dance.

'I spoke to him on the 'phone this morning. He's in love so I don't know how reliable his judgement is, but he assures me she's the most beautiful girl he's ever seen. I must admit Julian's always picked goodlookers.'

'So have you!'

'I admit to a weakness for beautiful women and beautiful horses.' He sniffed, 'You smell nice.'

'I'm wearing Pieter's perfume – he says it makes the hair curl on the men's chests.'

He rubbed his chest. 'I wondered what that tickling sensation was.' He took his eye off the road to look at me 'I like your dress. I've noticed you wear subtle colours, and always look elegant.'

'That's because I'm too thin,' I sighed. 'I wish I had a bosom like Marianna's.'

He laughed. 'I can't imagine you with her bosom – it wouldn't suit your personality.' He looked at me with a grin. 'I'm glad you haven't got her bosom,' he said softly. 'I like you as you are.'

We turned up the road skirting Mooi Vlei and saw Ellie, *Tant'* Bettie's little housemaid sitting on the fence. She was talking to Adonis who leant indolently against the fence looking up at her while he gently stroked her thigh, his hand half-way up her skirt.

Johan braked and we stopped in a cloud of dust. He put his head through the window. 'Adonis, you *vabond*! Come here,' he shouted angrily.

Adonis whispered to her and sauntered over to us, hips swinging and a broad smile on his light-skinned face. He took off his hat. 'Good-evening, *Baas* Johan.' He looked at me and bobbed his head. 'Good-evening *Klein Nooi*.'

I inclined my head coldly.

'Adonis,' Johan said sternly. 'I thought I told you to stay away from here.'

'But, *Baas* Johan!' His voice was falsetto and his eyebrows raised in outraged innocence. 'I'm jes on my way to see Jan September. *Baas* Johan know Jan September what live down this road. Now, when I come around the corner I see Ellie sitting on the fence and I jes stop to say a few words.'

Johan stared at him angrily. 'All right, get in. I'll give you a lift to Jan September.'

'Thank you, my *baas*.' He opened the door and clambered into the back of the car holding his hat. He stank of liquor, woodsmoke and sweat.

Ellie sat on the fence and watched us drive away.

'I'm warning you for the last time!' Johan said over his shoulder. 'Keep away from that girl! D'you hear me, Adonis? *Baas* Gert says if he finds you on his farm he'll shoot you so full of holes you'll look like a sieve.'

'Hêh! Hêh! Hêh!' Adonis laughed loudly with such infectious gaiety that against my will my lips curved in an involuntary smile. '*Baas* Gert not shoot straight! I watch him shoot guinea-fowl. They run and fly away, but not one drop dead. Not one, *Baas* Johan!'

92

'Be careful I don't help him.' Johan said without smiling. 'You know I can shoot straight.'

'Hêh! Hêh! Hêh! Yes, I know you shoot straight, my *Baas* – but I know you not shoot Adonis.'

Johan's lips twitched. 'You're a *skelm*! One day you'll land yourself in big trouble. Now you keep away from that girl – d'you hear me!'

'But, *Baas* Johan! I keep telling you all the time I'm jes talking to her.'

Johan slowed down, stopped the car and Adonis got out and stood next to the window, his flexible mouth curling. 'Thank you for the lift, my *Baas*. Good-night, *Baas* Johan. Good-night, *Klein Nooi*.' He put on his hat and walked away, whistling loudly.

'He's incorrigible!' Johan grinned.

I angrily fanned the air, trying to get rid of the rank smell. 'How can you smile, Johan! He's despicable and horrible – he's everything I loathe! It ruins my day just to see him.'

'Good Lord, Anna. You sounded like Ma!' He reached across and put his hand over mine and smiled. 'You won't let it spoil tonight, will you?' He swung the car off the road on to a grassy patch, switched off the engine and took me in his arms.

When we stopped at the Norths' house most of the guests had arrived and the big room was crowded. After we'd greeted Marianna and her husband, Johan took my arm and led me over to Julian, who was standing in the middle of the room. They shook hands with impulsive warmth and burst out laughing.

'So you're caught at last!' Johan smiled, clapping his back.

'Hook, line and sinker: I didn't have a hope from the moment I saw her. Wait until you've seen her – then you'll know why!'

93

'Where is she?' Johan looked around the room.

'Upstairs. She'll be down in a few minutes.'

Someone gently pinched my bottom. I turned and found *Oom* Gert smiling at me, his forehead glistening with tiny beads of perspiration. '*Magtig!* Anna! You're looking so pretty I hardly recognized you.'

Johan took my arm. 'See you later, Julian. Come, Anna, let's move out of this crush and find somewhere we can breathe.'

As we crossed the room I nudged him and he looked at me enquiringly. 'What is it?'

'*Oom* Gert's just pinched my bottom,' I said with a proud smile.

He laughed and slipped his arm around my waist. 'I've always told you not to underestimate yourself.' He tightened his arm. 'May I have the first dance?' I blushed and nodded.

He led me to the staircase and we leaned against the banisters, his arm still around my waist. I looked guiltily to see if Martin had arrived.

The coloured band struck up and started to play with the verve and rhythm of their race, and my heart beat quickly. Johan's arm slipped from my waist and I looked at him expectantly.

In that second my happiness was shattered.

He was staring up the staircase, his eyes narrowed and his face pale. A slender girl stood on the landing beneath the glittering chandelier like the central figure on a stage. The brilliant light pinpointed her blue-black hair and dazzlingly white shoulders. She was so beautiful that my heart went cold.

She slowly descended, her hand resting lightly on the banisters. She raised her head and saw Johan; she faltered, then continued, her eyes never leaving his face. When she drew level with me, I saw that her peacock-blue wild silk dress exactly matched her enormous eyes.

I quickly looked at Johan. He was dead white and his narrowed eyes were gleaming. He looks like a predatory beast, I thought with sudden bitter hatred.

He moved towards her as she reached the bottom step and taking her in his arms swept her on to the floor. I remained crouched against the banisters like a wounded animal.

A touch on my arm made me tear my eyes from them. 'Hallo Anna,' Martin smiled. 'Would you care to dance?' I mutely nodded, unable to smile. 'When did you arrive?' he asked. 'I got your message not to pick you up and came straight here.'

'We arrived half an hour ago.' My voice sounded flat and strained.

I kept my face pressed against his cheek and stared in front of me, trying not to look at Johan and Sarah, but when the music stopped we were standing next to them.

Julian pushed past us. 'There you are, Sarah! I've been looking for you everywhere.' He grinned. 'Trust Johan to find you!' When the music started he put his arm around her and Johan turned away and walked through the French door.

As the evening progressed my head began aching. The slightest movement was excruciating pain and ultimately it became intolerable. 'Martin, d'you mind if we don't dance? My head's aching. Could we sit outside? Perhaps the fresh air will help.'

His thin sensitive face was concerned. 'Of course. You're looking very pale. Would you like me to take you home?'

'No. I'd just like to sit quietly.'

He took my arm and we walked slowly to the end of the lawn. There was a small summer-house to the left and he led me into it. 'Let's see if we can find a bench in here,' he kept his grip on my arm. We found a curved seat and I gratefully sank down, gently probing and massaging the base of my skull, trying to ease the bunched muscles. Martin held my hand and we sat in silence.

A couple drifted across the lawn towards us. I immediately recognized Johan's tall silhouette and a shaft of light revealed the iridescent blue of Sarah's dress. They walked apart without speaking. When they reached the end of the lawn they turned and faced each other. She placed her hands on his shoulders, and with sudden violence he drew her to him, kissing her with such passion that her back arched. She folded her arms around his neck and clung to him. The kiss seemed to last for ever. Then he slowly released her and without speaking they turned and went back to the house.

'What's going on?' Martin whispered. 'Wasn't that Johan and Julian's fiancée?'

'Yes,' I said dully.

He gave a long low whistle. 'Good Lord!'

I shivered. 'Please take me home.'

I didn't feel the hot searing pangs of jealousy. I was cold with utter despair, as though I were dying.

'I had to speak to Bella,' Trina said at breakfast the next morning. 'It's becoming too much of a good thing. She never leaves Lettie alone for a second. She calls the child every filthy and unprintable name under the sun. They scream and shout at each other all day.' She looked at Johan. 'I hope you won't have trouble with them when we're gone.'

'I hope not,' he said without looking up.

'Bella has her faults but I can trust her – and Bettie has promised to keep an eye on things while we're away.' She poured the coffee and passed my cup. 'Have you packed your things, darling?' I shook my head. 'You know how limited we are in weight. I find suits and blouses the best answer. Especially as the weather's so unreliable. Here's your coffee, Johannes.' She handed the cup to him. She seemed unaware that we were both unusually silent. 'I don't use the word beauty lightly, but I must admit that girl Julian's marrying is beautiful. Don't you agree, Anna?'

'She's very beautiful,' I mumbled.

'I don't think I've seen a lovelier girl. Don't you agree, Johannes?'

'Yes, Ma.'

'Of course, all Bettie's geese are swans. She says Sarah's not only beautiful but also capable, sweet-tempered and artistic.'

He looked up. 'You make her sound a veritable paragon of virtue.' He caught my eye and winked. I looked at him stonily.

'Julian's done very well for himself! He's stopped gallivanting and is sensible enough to settle down. It's high time you thought of doing the same thing, Johannes. Why don't you find yourself a charming girl like Sarah?'

Oh, Trina, Trina, you said all the wrong things that morning.

He stirred his coffee and grinned amiably. 'I'll try, Ma.'

'It's really time you settled down. You can't spend your life gallivanting and running after girls.'

'What about *Oupa*?'

'Don't talk to me about that man! Your grandfather was a disgrace to the family!' she glared at him. 'Because of his irresponsibility your poor father had to work too hard all his life.'

'Well,' he pushed his chair back, 'I must be off.' He looked at me. 'Are you coming?'

'No,' I said curtly.

Trina looked at me with sharp surprise as he went out of the room. 'Are you ill, darling? You're looking very pale.'

'I've a splitting headache,' I muttered, putting a hand to my brow. Close to tears, I picked up Chiang. 'I think I'll lie down.'

In my room I put Chiang on my bed and walked to the window, staring unseeingly at Trina's garden. I heard Isabella miaow in the passage; I opened the door and she came in and rubbed against my legs, purring loudly; then leapt on to my bed, put a paw on Chiang's neck and washed his face.

Chapter Fourteen

FOR WEEKS I had dreaded the thought of leaving Wonderkloof. Now that the time was drawing near every
nerve in my being stretched to breaking point in my
impatience to escape and put half the world between
Johan and me. When I allowed myself to think of him I
remembered his pale tense face and lustful shining eyes.
I remembered the wild passion of his embrace when he
clasped Sarah in his arms.

'I hate him!' I thought with deep bitterness. 'How
despicable he is! He's a womanizer like his grandfather
and capable of betraying his best friend!'

My only regret at leaving Wonderkloof was to be
parted from Chiang. Instinct told him that I was leaving.
For days he followed me like a shadow, never letting me
out of his sight. He no longer cocked his head or wagged
his tail when I put him on my bed and spoke to him. He
lay with his muzzle resting on the counterpane regarding
me with sad reproachful eyes. I felt as though I too were
betraying my best friend.

Johan drove us to the Airport. At the last minute I
turned to him. 'Look after Chiang, Johan.'

'Wolf and I will look after him.'

'He's never slept alone.' My voice trembled.

He smiled. 'Don't worry, he'll sleep with me, though

I don't promise to allow him on my bed.' He kissed my cheek. 'Goodbye. Enjoy yourself. I'll miss you and Ma.' I walked away without looking back.

Uncle Charles and his wife, Elizabeth, met us at London Airport and we drove down to their home in Surrey. Trina had arranged to spend the first two days with them and then go up to London. Her plans were vague and mysterious.

'I've given you the number of my flat in Jermyn Street, darling. You'll be able to contact me there. I may go to the Continent but it will only be for a few days, and of course I'll write to you.' She chucked me under the chin. 'Cheer up, darling, and enjoy yourself! This is one of the loveliest parts of England and you're here in the spring.'

Uncle Charles was a tall shy man with my mother's hazel almond-shaped eyes. During the first two days while Trina was staying with them, he blinked and cleared his throat if she spoke to him. I noticed that when he did so she shifted in her seat and looked irritated. After she left, this nervous habit stopped.

'The Oaks', the home of my uncle and aunt, was a large stone house in Limpsfield Chart, near Oxted. It was a comfortable double-storeyed house with mullioned windows. The rooms had edge-to-edge carpeting and were unostentatiously furnished in bright colours, but the tones Aunt Elizabeth chose for her furnishing lacked the depth, warmth and subtlety of the curtains and carpets at Wonderkloof and it was also apparent that neither my uncle nor aunt were interested in antiques. Their furniture was good, solid, practical and hideous.

'It's deplorable,' Trina whispered before she left, 'that a well-to-do couple like Charles and Elizabeth should have such abominable taste!'

But Aunt Elizabeth loved her home and everything in it. 'This big house should have been full of children,' she said sadly. 'It's been a source of sadness to Charles and me that we've no family.'

She was a tall woman with a craggy, droll face. When she smiled she screwed up her blue eyes until they almost disappeared. In repose the humorous lines at the corners of her eyes were deeply etched. She wore good tweeds and expensive cashmere jerseys – but in spite of this, never looked well dressed.

Twice weekly a char cleaned the house and once a week an elderly woman from the village came in to do the ironing. Aunt Elizabeth was on intimate and friendly terms with both of them. We often sat in the kitchen and had tea with them at eleven o'clock, when they regaled her with the local gossip and the latest news of their families.

'Charles can afford to let me keep a full-time servant but I've told him I don't want one,' she said while efficiently setting about preparing our lunch. 'The last servant we had lived with us for fiteen years and made my life a misery. I don't intend to go through that again.' She added salt and pepper and vigorously stirred the contents of the pot. 'Now we eat when we feel like it – and eat what we like, not what the servant likes! When you do things for yourself you find the short cuts – you learn to do everything with the minimum amount of fuss and bother.' I watched fascinated, as she briskly chopped up the chives. 'Now when we've guests for dinner I no longer have to contend with a sour face and an unpleasant atmosphere in my own home. Instead of a cook, we've a full-time gardener. We find this a more satisfactory arrangement. He keeps the lawns cut and looks after the vegetables. Charles and I spend every minute we can in the garden, nevertheless it's impossible to keep down the weeds.'

The smooth rounded verge of the lawn was like emerald green velvet edged with great banks of rhododendrons burgeoned with heavy clusters of flowers. A grove of sycamores grew on the edge of the property. A hedge of pale yellow scented azaleas hid the kitchen garden where Hammet, the gardener, was usually at work, whistling softly while he tended his vegetables or set out the seedlings in the greenhouse. He was a surly young man who rarely smiled, and reminded me of a young white edition of *Ou* Attie.

'Hammet's an excellent gardener,' Aunt Elizabeth said. 'When he first came to work for me everybody told me I'd never keep him. But I've learned how to handle him.' She smiled and crinkled her eyes. 'I must never give him an order – it must be a tactfully worded suggestion.'

Uncle Charles was a partner in a firm of solicitors in London. When he left in the morning, he wore a dark suit and a bowler hat and invariably took his rain coat and umbrella. In the evening I accompanied him on his tour around the garden. He pointed out the rock and alpine plants which grew in the dry walls and flourished amongst the stones along the artificial stream which skirted the lawn. Spiky silver cushions of thrift sent up diminutive stemmed powder puffs of pale pink. 'And look, here's a white variety growing in this crevice.' I saw tight little blankets of red saxifrage. Uncle Charles showed me at least a dozen varieties of this plant peeping amongst the rocks and filling the crevices. Pink and mauve alpine phlox dripped over the edges of the walls mingling with pale watery blue campanulas. I saw gentians as brilliantly blue as Sarah's eyes. In the fields he introduced me to the humble buttercup with its shiny lacquered yellow petals.

We went for long drives through the counties of

Surrey, Sussex and Kent. The skies were usually leaden but the fields and hills vividly green, and everywhere I looked I saw majestic trees. These great trees of England impressed me more than anything I saw. The trees – and the lush virginal greenness of the hills and fields. I was enraptured by the great beeches and oaks soaring into the skies; by the immense horse-chestnuts bearing their candelabras of white flowers, and the billowing burgundy copper beeches. I'd never seen such ancient beautiful trees and each day looked at them with reverence and joy.

The days and weeks slipped by. The happy companionship with my uncle and aunt and the serenity and beauty of the English countryside healed my wounds and revived my spirits. Now, when I thought of Johan, it was no longer with bitterness or hatred.

Uncle Charles reminded me a great deal of my mother. He had her eyes and her gift for quiet companionship.

'It makes me so happy to see how well you and Charles get on.' Aunt Elizabeth said one morning. 'You're good for him, Anna. He's taken on a new lease of life.' She smiled. 'How much he'd love to have a daughter like you. Did you know that he was devoted to your mother?'

'He reminds me so much of her, I'm sure they had a wonderful companionship.'

'They did. It hurt him very much that she'd never allow him to help her.'

'Mom was proud. She often told me that it was her besetting sin.'

One evening Aunt Elizabeth invited the couple from next door to dinner. 'He's an architect, a rather nice young man who lives with his mother, Lady Bates.'

I smiled. 'You don't have to invite rather nice young men to dinner for my sake.'

In her youth Lady Bates must have been a beautiful

girl, but in middle age, her cold sculptured face was marred by an expression of petulance and discontent.

Her son, Oliver, had inherited her blonde hair, blue eyes and classical features. But there the likeness ended. Nothing could have been less apt than Aunt Elizabeth's description of Oliver being 'a rather nice young man'. He had a pair of piercing pale blue eyes. His face was lean, intelligent and hard. His well-cut dark suit fitted his rangy body with casual elegance.

He telephoned me a few days later and invited me over to his study after dinner. It was a bright and airy panelled room with built-in bookcases on both sides of the fireplace. The sofa and two chairs were covered in dull red and the curtains, which hung to the floor, were patterned in dark green, old gold and the same mellow red. His big desk, cluttered with papers and plans, stood next to the window.

He saw me looking at an abstract painting above the fireplace, a composition in black, red and white. Startling, fluid and disturbing. 'Well, what d'you think of it?'

'What's it meant to be?'

His eyebrows twitched irritably. 'What does it convey to you?'

'Nothing. What's it supposed to be?'

'For God's sake, Anna, must everything have to be something? Must everything have a meaning? Hasn't it any message for you?' He strode to the bookcase. 'Here's a book on modern art. Take it and read it tonight and try to improve your mind.' He glanced at me. 'Sit down, for God's sake.' He was blasphemous, rude and intolerant.

After this I often spent the evening in his study. 'Where's your mother?' I asked one night. 'I never see her.'

'Mother?' He stretched out his legs and leaned back. 'She's having an affair.'

'Really, Oliver!'

'Don't misunderstand me, my dear girl. Mother's had an affair at the bridge table for nearly thirty years, which left her little time to spend with her husband and son.' He paused. 'My father was fortunate. He found consolation elsewhere.'

'But what about you? Were you very lonely?'

He drew up his legs. 'Don't start that goddamned sentimental twaddle.'

'Were you?' I persisted.

He stared moodily in front of him. 'I was as lonely as hell.'

A few days before Trina was due to return Uncle Charles invited me to his study. 'Your Aunt won't need your help with the dinner tonight. She knows I'm going to talk to you and she also knows what I'm going to say. Sit down, my dear Anna, and make yourself at home.' I sank into the big easy chair opposite his desk and watched him fill his pipe. He tamped down the tobacco, struck a match and puffed until it was lit; then sat forward, leaning on his desk. 'Anna, Elizabeth and I have grown very fond of you. We were only saying today how we wished you were our daughter and how much we'll miss you when you leave.' He sat back and smiled at me. 'We want you to know that this place will one day be yours. We're leaving everything we have to you.' Deeply moved, I was unable to do more than murmur incoherently. 'We hope you'll often stay with us and look upon this as your second home.' He paused and carefully placed his pipe on the ashtray. 'If you should ever wish to live with us, I can assure you there's nothing that could bring us greater happiness.'

'Oh, Uncle Charles,' I sobbed. I jumped up and ran around his desk to kiss him and he put his arms around me and held me close.

The night before Trina returned I spent the evening with Oliver. When I came into his study he hardly greeted me and sat crouched over his desk for two hours. Later I made coffee and only then did he join me on the sofa. 'You leave in two days. My dear mother tells me we're dining at The Oaks tomorrow night.'

I moved uncomfortably, thinking how effusively welcoming and over-friendly Aunt Elizabeth was whenever she met Oliver; she had visions of us falling in love, marrying and living in the cottage next door.

He looked at me and gave one of his rare smiles, showing very white, even teeth. 'You know, Anna, you're nothing much to look at, but you've got one of the most transparent faces I've seen. Everything you think and feel is reflected in that little face of yours.'

'What's reflected in it now?'

'You're thinking of your dear Aunt Elizabeth.' I blushed. He took my chin and turned my face to his so that I was compelled to look into his clear blue eyes. 'Now there's consternation! You're frightened I'm going to kiss you. Don't worry, I've no intention of doing so.' He sat back and sipped his coffee. 'Will you be coming to stay with your Uncle and Aunt again?'

'Yes, probably.'

He glanced at me with a slight smile. 'Good. I look forward to continuing our acquaintance.'

'You're quite different, Anna,' Trina said, 'I thought you were very peaked and pale when we left. Are the headaches any better?'

'Much better.' I smiled.

I was delighted to see her. She looked well and extremely elegant in a new wine-coloured woollen suit.

'I can't understand it. You've never suffered from headaches before. If they don't improve your eyes must

106

be tested when we get back to Cape Town.' She turned to Uncle Charles. 'Oh, Charles, before I forget! James will be fetching us tomorrow so you won't have the fuss and bother of driving us up to London.' He blinked nervously and cleared his throat. She opened her bag and took out her cigarette case. 'I've had only one letter from Johannes. If it hadn't been for Bettie I wouldn't know what's been happening at Wonderkloof. Pieter has written to me every week.'

'Oh, Trina!' Aunt Elizabeth exclaimed, dismayed. 'I'm so sorry, I forgot to tell you that a letter arrived for you this morning. It's on the hall table.' She looked at me. 'Anna, dear. Won't you fetch it.'

It was lying on the silver tray on the hall table. I picked it up and recognized Johan's firm handwriting. In five days I'd be back at Wonderkloof and with him. 'Here's a letter from Johan, Trina.'

'And high time too! Johannes has always been a poor correspondent.' She looked at the envelope, then opened her bag and took out her spectacles. 'Forgive me, Charles and Elizabeth, if I read this.'

'Do. I should have given it to you when you arrived.' Aunt Elizabeth smiled at me. 'Have you finished your packing, dear?'

'I haven't even started – but it won't take long.'

Trina gave a sudden explosive exclamation and I looked at her in amazement. She crushed the letter in her hand.

I shall always remember that moment. Her brown eyes blazing with anger and the crisp crackling sound of the paper as she crumpled it fiercely in her fist.

'What's wrong?' I asked breathlessly. 'What's happened?'

She looked at me, her cheeks flushed with rage. 'Johannes is married!'

Chapter Fifteen

I HAD FIVE days in which to adjust myself. Five days in which I must learn to face the fact that the dreams and hopes I'd held for the future no longer existed. The memories I'd so fondly cherished must now be buried; the hopes forgotten. I never consciously allowed myself to think of Johan. By sheer strength of mind I tried to kill my love for him. They always write of the agony of first love and that it dies hard, I whispered to myself in the middle of the night, clenching my fists. But I'll kill it, I'll kill it!

London. The dinner with Colonel Jamieson at the Savoy. The trip to Paris. All had an unreal dreamlike quality in which I moved like an automaton. I was grimly fighting my lonely battle.

During those days I was silent, apathetic and distrait, suffering from constant blinding headaches. Trina often touched my arm and looked at me anxiously. 'Oh, darling, you look so ill! You've a headache again. We must do something about it as soon as we get home. You can't go on like this.'

She didn't mentioned Johan's marriage until we were on the flight from Johannesburg to Cape Town. She appeared to be reading, then put her book face down on her lap and removed her spectacles. 'I've accepted

Johannes' marriage,' she said, turning to me. 'As you know, I've been telling him it's high time he settled down.' She shrugged expressively. 'Well, now he's done so!' She changed her position to face me directly. 'But I must confess I find it hard to forgive him for the way he's done it.' Her face was hard and censorious. 'Firstly, the indecent and unseemly haste, and secondly, that he should marry Julian's fiancée – the intended bride of his best friend. This I find impossible to understand and even more difficult to forgive.' She shook her head. 'How will I face Bettie and Gert? They're my oldest and closest friends. You'd never know, Anna, what a wonderful friend Bettie has been to me.' She opened her bag and took out her cigarette case. As she lit a cigarette I saw her hand trembling. 'Those terrible days after Jan was killed – only she knows the anguish and despair I suffered. Only she knows of my loneliness and tears. She put an arm around me and stood by me during that time as steadfastly as a rock.' She paused. 'It upsets me more than I can say that my son should cause her unhappiness. Julian was deeply in love with Sarah and I know how much Bettie will suffer with him.' She drew a deep breath. 'It wouldn't surprise me if she never wanted to see me again.'

'But, Trina, *Tant* Bettie could never blame you.'

'He's my son,' she said, lifting her chin and speaking with quiet dignity. 'Johannes and Julian spent their childhood at Mooi Vlei and Wonderkloof, running in and out of both houses. Julian's been as close as a brother to him and Bettie loved him like a second mother.' Her eyes were dark and distressed. 'How could he do this to them? How could he!'

'I don't think he could help it,' I said in a low voice.

She looked at me with a quick twist of her head. 'Why d'you say that?'

'He fell in love with Sarah the moment he saw her.' I paused and swallowed. 'And she fell in love with him.'

'How can you possibly know this, Anna?'

'I was there when it happened.'

The look she gave me was uncomfortably penetrating. 'Oh, I see.' I averted my face and stared out of the window. 'Well,' she said after a prolonged silence. 'It's no use crying over spilt milk. It's done, and nothing will change it. We must hope that Julian will find it in his heart to forgive Johannes and that in time Gert and Bettie will forgive us.'

The plane lost height and I knew that within twenty minutes we would land in Cape Town. The palms of my hands were damp and my pulse quickened. Coldly I forced my mind to remain blank.

Johan and Sarah stood at the fence next to the gateway. I looked at him and felt nothing. I was even able to smile inwardly at the wary expression on his face.

'You're looking well, Johannes,' Trina said as she pulled his head down to kiss him. She turned quickly and kissed Sarah lightly on the cheek. 'How kind of you, my child, to come with Johannes.'

'I had to come, Mrs de Villiers.' Her voice was deep-pitched and intense. 'I know how angry you must be. I felt I must be with Johan when he met you.' She glanced at him and smiled; then took his hand and held it tightly. Her beauty was radiant and flawless.

Trina's eyes flashed. 'You've both behaved abominably!' Then her face softened and she smiled. 'But I'm not going to scold you.' She rummaged in her handbag. 'Here are the tickets, Johannes. Will you please collect our baggage.' She held out the tickets and turned to Sarah. 'You can't call your mother-in-law Mrs de Villiers, my child. You'd better call me Trina – everyone does.'

110

Chiang was waiting for us in the car; I saw his black face looking through the window and my heart leapt. 'Oh, Johan, you've brought Chiang! I'm so pleased.'

'I knew how you'd be longing to see him.'

When I clasped him to me Chiang wriggled, snuffled and cried hysterically. He lay relaxed in my arms on the way to Wonderkloof.

After dinner we were sitting in front of the fire, when the sound of the door opening made me look up and I saw *Oom* Gert and *Tant'* Bettie entering the room. Trina put her coffee cup on the sofa table and stood up, a slight flush on her cheeks.

Tant' Bettie hastily crossed the room and affectionately embraced her. '*Ag*, my dearest Trina, Gert and I felt we must come over and welcome you home.'

Oom Gert was close on her heels. 'Welcome home, Trina!' he cried, hugging her. '*Magtig!* How much we've missed you. The place isn't the same without you!' He gave her another bearlike hug and a noisy smacking kiss.

Trina stood very straight, her eyes suspiciously bright.

Tant' Bettie turned to me and folded me to her bosom. '*Ag*, my dearest little Anna. How nice to have you back with us.' She held me at arm's length and looked me up and down. 'But my child, how thin you've grown! Didn't they give you enough to eat in England?' Johan was ill at ease and strained. She stood on tiptoe and kissed him. 'Congratulations, Johan.' She turned to Sarah but didn't kiss her. 'And you too, Sarah. Gert and I wish you all the happiness in the world.' She walked over to Trina and took her arm. 'Now, Trina, come and sit with me on the sofa and tell me about your trip.'

Later that night, Trina tapped on my door. I was sitting on the edge of my bed playing with Chiang.

'I've come to see how you are. You've been so pale. Have you another one of those bad headaches?'

111

I gently massaged the nape of my neck. 'I took two tablets and feel better now.'

She kissed me and placed her cool hand on my forehead; then went over to the dressing-table and looked at herself in the mirror, automatically straightening her skirt. 'I hope you'll be fortunate enough to find as good a friend as Bettie.'

I picked up Chiang and joined her at the mirror and looked at our reflection; then smiled and kissed her. 'I *am* fortunate – I've one just as good!'

The following morning I drove over to spend the day with Maria. Winter had started and it was heavily overcast. By the time I reached Mooi Vlei the rain was pelting down and I ran up the steps with hunched shoulders and bent head. Maria was waiting for me in the hall and took me to her room.

She hugged me. 'Oh, it's nice to have you back! I've so much to tell you, I don't know where to start.' She sat on the stool in front of her dressing-table and I sat on the edge of her bed. Her eyes sparkled with excitement and she looked radiantly happy. 'First of all, John and I are getting married next month.'

'Next month!'

'Yes. He's been offered a wonderful job in Pretoria.' She shook her head sadly. 'It nearly breaks my heart to think of leaving the Cape. He has to start work at the end of next month: this means we've either got to marry then or wait until June next year. We discussed it and decided to get married on the fifteenth and would like you to be one of my bridesmaids.' I nodded and smiled. 'Mom and I bought the material for your dress in Cape Town last week. Will you come here next Monday morning? The dressmaker's coming and will fit you when she's finished with me.'

'I can't believe you'll be married so soon,' I said sadly, knowing how much I'd miss her.

'There was a great drama two days after you and *Tant'* Trina left. Sarah swept into the dining-room when we were at breakfast and announced that the engagement was off – her bags were packed and she said she was returning to Johannesburg. I felt sorry for Julian: he was absolutely stunned! He was madly in love with her. He's always fallen for beautiful girls and Sarah's the most beautiful one I've ever seen.'

'I agree,' I muttered.

She puckered her brow. 'You know, Anna, I couldn't take to her. She spent hours in front of her dressing-table staring at herself. When she first came she put herself out to be charming to everyone. Not that she was particularly civil to me: she obviously considered me to be of little importance.' She grinned. 'You can imagine what Dad was like – absolutely besotted!' Her smile vanished. 'You've never seen such a transformation as took place the morning she walked into the dining-room and told us that she was leaving. She was unpleasant and downright rude. Poor Julian had to drive her to the airport. Mom was very upset: she cried, but later I heard her say to Dad, "Gert, I'm glad Julian's not marrying that girl – I don't think she'd make him happy." Three weeks later when we heard that Johan had married Sarah in Johannesburg, she was so furious she forgot to cry. Poor Julian – he went quite white. Did you know that Mom's sent him to Europe? He'll be away about four months.' She avoided my eyes. 'I didn't write when we heard they were married. I knew you'd hear sooner or later.'

When I drove back to Wonderkloof it was still raining. I found Trina and Martin sitting in front of the fire.

She looked up and smiled. 'Martin dropped in to see you and is staying to dinner.' Later that night she tapped on my door. I was reading in bed and Chiang lay in the crook of my arm. She kissed me. 'Good-night, darling.' When she reached the door she looked back. 'I like Martin Joubert – he's a good boy.'

Chapter Sixteen

THE NEXT MORNING Trina drove me to Cape Town to have my eyes tested and fetch Pieter from boarding-school.

The oculist examined me thoroughly. 'I can find nothing wrong with her eyes, Mrs de Villiers. Her vision's perfect.' He looked at me questioningly. 'You say these headaches have only started recently?'

'They started about two months ago,' I mumbled, looking down and fidgeting.

He turned to Trina. 'It may be advisable to take her to a physician for a check up. The fact that there's no history of migraine in either family and that there've previously been no headaches may be an indication of something wrong.' He put his elbows on the desk and placed his finger tips together. 'Has anything been worrying you?' I shook my head. He smiled kindly. 'No economic worries – or unhappy love affairs?'

'Her mother died a year ago,' Trina interrupted quickly. 'They were very close.'

'Ah.' He stroked his chin and studied me. 'That could be a contributing factor.' He cleared his throat and rose. 'Well, Mrs de Villiers, my advice to you is to take her to see a physician if the headaches don't improve.' We shook hands and he saw us to the door.

I turned to Trina as we walked down the passage. 'I won't see a physician!'

As always, she was unpredictable. I'd steeled myself for an argument, but she merely patted my arm without looking at me and said nothing.

Pieter was sitting on the low brick wall in front of the school. He jumped off when he saw us and came to the car. He had grown over an inch since I'd seen him and was tall and gangling and had difficulty controlling his huge feet. His face was more bony and his lips full and slightly puffy.

'Gee, Ma,' he said as he clambered awkwardly into the car. 'Weren't you surprised when you heard Johan was married?'

'Surprised is putting it mildly.'

'She's a real smasher! All the fellows in my class want to come to Wonderkloff for the September holidays.'

'How d'you know she's a smasher – as you so vulgarly put it?'

'She and Johan came to see me on Sunday three weeks ago.'

'Oh, that was good of Johannes. Sometimes he can be surprisingly considerate.'

'You should have seen the boarders hanging around when they brought me back.' He chuckled. 'Gee, Ma, I've never been so popular! Even the Matric boys were all over me. I've promised to take pictures of her during the holidays. I'll make a super selection and flog them when I get back.'

'Flog them?' she frowned. 'What does that expression mean?'

'Sell them, Ma,' he prodded me stealthily in the back. 'I'm sorry it's winter – I'll be able to charge more for the ones of her in a bikini.'

116

'I forbid it!' she cried outraged. 'D'you hear me, Pieter? I absolutely forbid it!'

The next morning after breakfast Johan and Sarah left the dining-room with Pieter close on their heels and I followed Trina into the kitchen. Lettie was at the sink washing up, her body clumsy and unmistakably pregnant.

'Lettie,' Trina said. 'Go up to my room and do it at once. I may want to lie down in half an hour.'

Lettie looked at her sullenly, dried her hands and went out of the room.

'Don't you feel well?' I asked.

She waved her hand vaguely. 'Bella, what arrangements have been made about Lettie's baby? She must be due in seven or eight weeks. Have clothes, nappies and blankets been bought? And who's going to help her when her time comes?'

Bella's body seemed to swell. She folded her hands over her stomach and pursed her lips. 'It not my business, *Merrem*,' she said harshly.

'Of course it's your business! Whatever Lettie's done and however angry you are with her, she's still your daughter.'

'She no daughter of mine! She a low class street girl.' Her voice rose. 'If there nobody what help her it her fault. The Lord punish her for bringing shame on her mother what treat her so good.'

'Are you telling me that you'll do nothing to help her?'

'No!' she shouted violently. 'No! I not do anything to help her! Why should I? She got no gratitude for what her mother done.' She drew a deep breath. 'I wish she go!' she cried shrilly. 'So I don't see her again!'

'Very well, Bella.' Trina turned to me. 'Come, Anna.' She walked quickly out of the kitchen, muttering under her breath. We found Lettie making up the bed. 'Lettie,'

Trina said quietly. 'Have you bought clothes, nappies and blankets for your baby? Have you made any plans?'

Lettie didn't look up. 'No, *Ou Nooi*.'

'Why not?' Trina asked, a shade impatiently.

Lettie's face was expressionless. 'I got no money, *Ou Nooi*. Mammie take all my money. When I ask for something for the baby she shout and hit me. I frightened to ask again.'

Trina sighed loudly. 'I'll buy things for your baby – don't worry.' She smiled at Lettie kindly. 'I'll speak to Christina – *Ou* Attie's daughter,' she explained to me – 'and arrange for her to take you into her cottage at the end of the month. She'll help you when the baby's born.'

There was a long pause. 'Yes, *Ou Nooi*,' Lettie muttered ungraciously. She looked at Trina with no sign of gratitude.

Winter started early that year. The north-west gales swept across the farm uprooting trees, to be followed by heavy rains.

The following week I took Chiang for a walk. It was a cold blustery day with intermittent showers. As soon as he saw me take my thick woollen coat from the cupboard he spun in tight circles and barked excitedly. He was now able to go long distances without tiring. We went through the court-yard and I opened the gate on the farm-yard. In spite of my shouts, he chased a scrawny hen nearly having her by the tail feathers. He slunk back looking guilty, and I picked him up and spanked him soundly.

We turned off the farm-yard and went down the path towards the *volks'* cottages. He was running ahead, when suddenly he stopped in his tracks and looked sharply to the right, wagging his tail. A moment later

118

Johan and Sarah emerged from the pine forest on the right of the *volks'* cottages and walked up the footpath towards me. Sarah was in front carrying a basket. She wore a blue coat and a blue Paisley scarf tied under her chin. Wolf was at Johan's heels. He stopped and pricked his ears then loped swiftly up the hill and briefly licked Chiang's face.

I waited for them to join me and opened my mouth to speak when a single piercing scream splintered the silence and froze us to shocked immobility. Another rending shriek lashed my nerves like a whip.

Johan leapt forward, ran down the path with Wolf at his heels and disappeared around the corner. I snatched up Chiang who was in pursuit, and followed them. Sarah was in front of me and momentarily obscured my vision – and then I saw Annekie.

She was lying in the middle of the path, her body arched and her hands clasped over her belly in a pathetic attempt to protect herself. Adonis stood above her, his face livid as he brutally kicked her in the stomach.

I stopped, gasping and instinctively clutched Chiang protectively.

Each time Adonis kicked her I could hear the sickening dull thud of his boot sinking into her flesh. She screamed agonizingly and his face convulsed in a spasm of hatred. He shouted at her calling her a filthy name and crashed his boot into her face.

I cried out, clapping my hand over my mouth to prevent myself from screaming.

At that moment Johan reached him. He caught Adonis by the shoulder and spun him around. I hardly saw the movement of his arm but I heard the sharp crack as his fist connected with Adonis' jaw. He threw up his arms, reeling backwards, tripped over Annekie and fell on his back. Silently and swiftly as an arrow Wolf flew at him and buried his teeth in his throat. Adonis' hoarse guttural scream was more blood-chilling than Annekie's final shriek.

'Wolf!' Johan's voice was like a whiplash. In one stride he had the dog by his thick ruff. Wolf immediately let go, and Johan slapped him sharply across the muzzle with the flat of his hand. 'Heel!' Wolf slunk behind him.

As Adonis rose from the mud Johan stepped forward and put out a hand to help him. 'Let me see your throat, Adonis.'

Adonis looked at him like a snarling animal, his sensual lips drawn from his teeth. His face was murderous. He struck Johan's hand away. 'Don't touch me, my *Baas*!' he said savagely, breathing quickly. 'Don't ever touch me again!'

He slowly beat the mud from his clothing; then picked up his hat and walked away without looking at us.

Annekie rolled over and painfully got to her knees, her head hanging between her arms. She tried to rise and Johan took her arms and heaved her to her feet. She recoiled as though he were a leper. She swayed in front of us with glazed eyes and slowly wiped the back of her hand across her bleeding mouth and with an effort straightened her body. Dragging her feet and holding her hand to her side she limped down the path after Adonis. We stood and watched in silence until she disappeared around the corner.

'Darling!' Sarah cried exultantly. She ran to Johan and flung her arms around his neck and kissed him passionately. 'You were magnificent! I was so proud of you!'

He put up his hands and pulled her arms down, his face pale and set. 'I shouldn't have hit him.'

She took his hand and kissed it, holding it against her cheek. 'Of course you should have hit him, darling! That vile brute was murdering her!'

He withdrew his hand and put it to his mouth, gently sucking his skinned knuckles. 'There's no excuse. I shouldn't have hit him – no good will come of it.'

'I don't agree with you! You and Wolf were absolutely magnificent. You wonderful, wonderful dog.' She reached out to stroke him but he backed away, moving closer to Johan. She turned and seized his arm with both hands. 'Johan.' Her voice was low and vibrant. 'Why didn't you let Wolf kill him?'

'Are you mad!' I cried.

She'd forgotten my presence. Now she swung around to face me, her face dead white and her eyes blazing with excitement. 'No, I'm not mad! I mean every word. Kill him! Wolf should have torn that beast to pieces – I would have let him do it! If I'd had a gun in my hand I would have shot Adonis with no compunction – he's nothing but a vile vicious animal!' She turned back to Johan. 'Darling,' she said breathlessly. 'Why didn't you let Wolf kill him? Why didn't you?'

His face was emotionless. He took her arm. 'Come, darling, let's go home.'

When I told Trina what had happened, she looked stern. 'Johannes shouldn't have hit him!'

'But he deserved it!' I cried indignantly. 'He was kicking her to death.'

'That's not the point, my child. He could have stopped Adonis without hitting him.' She looked tired. 'Johannes struck him down in front of three women – but worst of all he did so in front of Annekie. Adonis will never forgive her for having seen this happen.' She paused and sighed. 'I only hope for her own sake, she never reminds him of it.'

121

Chapter Seventeen

I TRIED SO hard to fall in love with Martin. The willpower I'd employed to kill my love for Johan, I now directed with concentration and intensity into loving Martin.

I was able to look at Johan without a trace of feeling. There was no longer an urge to brush his unruly hair from his forehead; nor did my pulse quicken if he entered the room unexpectedly. We could speak naturally and were able to laugh together. I could sit back and regard him both dispassionately and critically. It was possible to meet my eyes in the mirror and say with conviction, 'I don't love him anymore.'

With the same grim determination I tried to project my thoughts in a flowing stream towards Martin. In the dark hours of the night I clenched my fists, whispering over and over again, I'll fall in love with him. I will! I'll make myself love him! But it didn't work. Having successfully killed my love for Johan, I also destroyed all feelings of warmth and emotion in myself.

When Martin kissed me I no longer derived pleasure from the soft warm contact of his mouth. In desperation I simulated passion I didn't feel. Encouraged and enflamed by my response, his mouth opened and he slipped his hand down the front of my dress and cupped my breast. I gasped and pushed him away.

'What is it, Anna? What's wrong, darling?'

He put his arms around me and tried to draw me to him but I put my palms against his chest and held him away. 'Oh, Martin, I'm sorry,' I said sadly. 'It won't work.'

He smiled. 'What won't work, darling?' Unable to answer him I sat in silence. He took my hands and kissed them, then drew me into his arms and laid his cheek against mine. 'You must know by now that I love you. I fell in love with you the first moment I saw you walk on to *Tant'* Bettie's *stoep* with your eyes full of tears.'

'I'm sorry, Martin.'

'Listen to me, I know it with absolute certainty.'

'I don't love you.'

'That will come.' He drew me closer. 'Let's get married,' he whispered hoarsely, his mouth against my ear. 'Let's get married now – at once! I swear I'll make you love me.'

I withdrew from the warmth and protection of his arms. 'It's hopeless. It will never work,' I said sadly. 'When you kiss me I feel nothing – nothing at all. I don't even like it.' I drew a shuddering breath. 'When you touch me as you did just now, I feel complete revulsion.'

He switched on the engine and put the car into gear. We drove in silence to Wonderkloof and when he stopped at the bottom of the steps I quickly jumped out and slammed the door, and he drove away without looking at me or saying goodbye.

Maria had a fine day for her wedding. She was married in the late afternoon and the reception was in the hall and spacious living-rooms of Mooi Vlei.

This was to be Johan and Sarah's first public appearance since their marriage – a marriage which had caused much gossip, speculation and criticism. She wore a

123

simple light-weight woollen suit matching her eyes. Her petalled close-fitting hat emphasized her faintly hollowed cheeks and the classic line of her jaw. The diamond and sapphire clasp of her pearls glittered against her white throat and a sapphire and diamond brooch was pinned to her lapel. She kept close to Johan and when they were parted her eyes seldom left his face.

The previous day Trina and I had helped *Tant'* Bettie arrange the flowers in the reception rooms.

'*Ag*, my child,' *Tant'* Bettie said, taking my hand and tucking it under her arm. 'When you think how hard we all worked yesterday and now the rooms are so crowded that no one even notices our lovely flowers.' Her face was hot and flushed, and she fanned herself vigorously. 'I'm so hot and uncomfortable,' she whispered. 'My new corsets are too tight – Maria wouldn't let me wear my old comfortable ones.' She looked at Maria. 'Doesn't she look lovely? And *Ag*! so happy.' She dabbed her eyes. 'I hope John will look after my little girl and keep her happy.'

An arm was slipped around my waist. 'How are you, Anna, my child?' *Oom* Gert said, kissing me and patting my shoulder, but he didn't pinch my bottom. I wasn't looking my best. The colour and style of the bridesmaid's dress didn't suit me and I knew I was pale and too thin. '*Magtig!* Doesn't Marianna look like a beautiful rose this afternoon?'

The description was apt. Her hat was a confection of fully-blown pink roses and darker pink stamens. Her sheath dress of pale pink lace was a stem from which rose the voluptuous twin mounds of her breasts, gleaming subtly like rosy alabaster.

She was talking to Johan, looking at him provocatively. She whispered something and he burst out laughing, his teeth startlingly white in his sun-tanned face. He lowered his head and spoke to her softly and she too laughed, patting his lean cheek.

Someone gripped my arm. I turned to find Sarah standing next to me. I was surprised because she rarely noticed my presence and seldom spoke to me. She was white around the mouth and her deep blue eyes were enormous.

'Who's that woman?' she whispered.

'What woman?' I stared at her.

'That dreadful vulgar creature speaking to Johan.'

I smiled. 'Surely you don't mean Marianna? That's Mrs North. Don't you remember her? You and Johan met at her dance. She's flirtatious and silly but quite harmless.' I grinned. 'She's always had a soft spot for Johan.'

'I hate her!' Her voice trembled with passion.

I looked at her incredulously. 'But Sarah! Marianna flirts with everyone. It doesn't mean a thing.'

'I hate her!' she repeated. 'She's nothing but a common trollop.' Deathly pale, her fingers were biting into my bare flesh.

Johan saw us staring at him. He smiled and taking Marianna's arm came over. 'Darling,' he said to Sarah, putting his arm around her. 'You remember Marianna North, don't you? You met two months ago.'

'Hallo, Sarah,' Marianna held out her hand. 'I remember you well.' She smiled. 'It wouldn't be easy to forget you.'

Sarah ignored her hand. Stony-faced, she deliberately looked Marianna up and down, then turned her shoulder. 'Darling,' she said to Johan. 'I'm so thirsty. D'you think you could find me something to drink? Preferably long, cold and non-alcoholic.'

The blood rushed to Marianna's cheeks and she dropped her hand; then, gracefully shrugging her magnificent shoulders, lifted her eyebrows significantly at Johan and turned away.

'What's wrong with you, Sarah?' He spoke quietly but his face was hard and his eyes gleamed with anger. 'Why were you so damned rude?'

'How dare you publicly humiliate me,' she hissed.

'What the devil are you talking about?'

'You know perfectly well what I'm talking about,' her voice was low and furious. 'How could you let that vulgar woman paw you all over.'

'For God's sake! What's the matter with you?'

'There's nothing the matter with me! You were disgusting!' Her eyes were blazing.

'Keep your voice down and pull yourself together!' He was now as pale with rage as she was.

'I won't keep my voice down. I'll speak exactly as I please.'

'Very well. Then I'll leave you until you've come to your senses.'

He turned on his heel but she caught his arm and pulled him back. 'I want you to take me home.'

'I'll take you home when the wedding's over,' he said stiffly.

'I want you to take me home now!' Her voice was perilously high.

People were turning around and staring at us. I saw Marianna watching from the other side of the room.

'Sarah,' I said softly.

'Shut up!' she shouted, turning on me like a wildcat.

Johan took her arm. 'Don't make a scene. Can't you see everyone's staring at us?'

'I don't care if they're staring. I'm warning you, Johan – if you don't take me home this instant I'll scream. I'll scream the place down!'

'Very well,' he said icily. 'I'll take you home.' His face

was like granite. Keeping his grip on her arm he steered her over to *Tant* Bettie. 'I'm taking Sarah home. She's not feeling well.'

'*Ag*, Sarah,' her face was concerned. 'I'm so sorry you're not well.' She looked at her searchingly. 'Go straight to bed when you get home, my child.' She kissed Johan, patting his arm and knowingly smiled. 'Look after her. Keep her quiet and don't let her do too much.'

I saw Maria beckoning and went to her. 'Come to my room and sit with me while I change.'

I undid her wedding-gown and hung it up. 'It's a beautiful dress, Maria. You looked lovely in it.'

I sat on the edge of her bed while she put on her going-away suit and then went to the dressing-table to make up her face. 'Martin telephoned John last week,' she said, touching up her eyebrows. 'He told him he wouldn't be coming to our wedding.' I remained silent. 'We were very hurt. Martin's one of our oldest friends. I could see John was upset so I 'phoned Martin this morning and tried to persuade him to change his mind – but he was adamant.' She turned around. 'Have you quarrelled by any chance?'

'No.' I avoided her eyes and picked at the fabric of my dress. When I looked up she was still staring at me. 'We're not seeing each other anymore.'

'Oh.'

I moved uncomfortably. 'It's no use, Maria. It couldn't work – I'm not in love with him. There was no future for him in our relationship.'

'No, I suppose not.' She put on her hat, drew on her gloves and snapped her handbag shut, facing me with sudden resolution. 'Anna, I know it's none of my business, but I'm fond of you.' She paused and smiled diffidently. 'Don't be upset by what I'm going to say,

127

or think I'm meddling in affairs which don't concern me. Don't you think it would be better if—'

'Don't say it!' I interrupted quickly. 'Don't say anything which might affect our friendship on this of all days.'

She continued to look at me then shrugged. 'If you come to Pretoria, we'll expect you to stay with us.' She kissed me quickly. 'Goodbye. I'll write to you.' I followed her to the door. On the threshold she turned and looked back. 'I hope things will work out for you.'

In the hall she tossed the bridal bouquet in my direction. I was the tallest girl in the group and caught it easily; but then, holding it awkwardly and twisting it in my fingers, I didn't know what to do with it. Later I hid it behind the copper vase in *Oom* Gert's study.

Chapter Eighteen

A FEW DAYS later Johan and Sarah left Wonderkloof to spend a week in Johannesburg.

Trina and I had drawn our chairs in front of the fire with the standard lamp between us.

'Fortunately Johannes can leave the farm at this time. It will do him good to have a holiday. He's not been himself these last few weeks. That business with Adonis has upset him more than he cares to admit. I'm so pleased he's able to fix my business affairs for me and I no longer have to go to Johannesburg. I don't enjoy staying there. The bustling tempo of that city's too much at my age.' She picked up a piece of wood and tossed it on to the fire. 'It will be nice for Sarah to see her friends and family. I know her parents aren't alive, but she tells me she has a brother living in Johannesburg.' She paused and looked at me. 'Would you like to invite Martin Joubert to spend next weekend at Wonderkloof?'

'No, thanks,' I said curtly.

She continued looking at me. 'You haven't been out with him for some time. Is he away?'

'No.' I glanced down and caressed Chiang's ears. 'We aren't going out anymore''

'Oh.' In the silence that followed I picked up my book and continued reading.

We read for half an hour, then she put her book on the table and laid her spectacles next to it. 'Next week, if the weather's fine, we'll prune the roses. Put some more wood on the fire, Anna. It's nearly out.' While I did so she yawned and stretched. 'Did I tell you that I had a letter from James today? He's returning next month. He's been in Bermuda and says his next book's nearly finished. He writes an entertaining letter. I'm so fond of him – I wish I could find his books more interesting.'

Isabella miaowed, sprang lightly on to my lap and started to wash Chiang's face. He opened his eyes and growled, then attacked her, barking and biting her until she jumped on to the floor.

Trina raised her eyebrows. 'Well I never! He's growing up and becoming bad-tempered.' She lit a cigarette and leant back, stretching her feet towards the fire which was crackling and burning brightly. 'I was thinking this morning that I must invite Mrs Fourie and her son to spend a weekend with us after James gets back. I've been meaning to ask them for some time.'

'Who are they?' I frowned and looked at her suspiciously. 'I've never heard of them.'

'They're charming. She's a widow and her son's a well-mannered young man. They own a farm in the Swellendam district.'

I put Chiang on the floor and sat on the edge of my chair. 'Trina, please don't invite him on my account. I'd find it most embarrassing to be thrown together with a strange man all weekend.' I glowered at her. 'I'd absolutely hate it!'

'Nonsense, darling,' she said calmly. He's a charming boy – I know you'll like him.'

The night Johan and Sarah returned from Johannesburg, we were having dinner when a sudden commotion caused us to look up in surprise.

'What on earth's that racket about!' Trina said, reaching for the bell.

A moment later Bella burst in, wailing loudly, her cap awry and tears streaming down her cheeks.

Trina straightened her back. 'What's happened, Bella?'

'Oh, *Merrem*, it bad! It bad!' She wrung her hands and tried to speak, then picked up her apron, buried her face in it and burst into hysterical tears. 'Oh! Oh! Oh!'

'Bella!' Trina's voice was harsh. 'Pull yourself together and tell us what's happened.'

'Oh! Oh! Oh!' Bella lifted her wet black face from the folds of her apron. 'It bad, *Merrem*! It bad!' Her small eyes darted to each one of us to see if she held our attention. 'Five minutes ago Christina come to the kitchen, *Merrem*.' She paused dramatically and drew herself to her full height. 'She say Adonis murder Annekie!' She wailed again and hid her face in her apron.

'What happened, Bella? How did he kill her?' Johan asked quickly. He was leaning forward and his knuckles gleamed whitely as his hands gripped the arms of his chair.

'Oh, Massa Johan! He throw petrol over her – he throw petrol over her and set her alight and burn her alive.'

'Oh, no!' Trina's exclamation was a wounded cry. 'No!' She covered her face with her hands and bowed her head. When she looked up, her face was ravaged and she appeared old and shrunken. 'We must go to the cottages at once, Johannes,' she said quietly. 'We must see if there's anything we can do.' His face was like marble. Trina turned to Christina. 'Is it quite certain Annekie's dead?'

Christina and Lettie had followed Bella into the dining-room and were standing in the background.

Christina stepped forward. She was as black as her father, *Ou* Attie. She clasped her hands and held them against her mouth. 'Yes, *Ou Nooi*, she dead! She dead! She burn like a candle, *Ou Nooi*, and all the time she burn she scream – and scream!' Her eyes rolled back and she gave a piercing shriek, clapping her hands over her ears as if to shut out the sound of Annekie's screams.

Trina pushed her chair back and jumped to her feet. 'We must go, Johannes!'

'I'll be ready in five minutes, Ma. I'll light the lanterns and have the jeep waiting.' Sarah took his arm and they left the room.

Trina turned to me. 'Anna, will you run upstairs and fetch my thick coat and a woollen scarf.'

I brought them and found her waiting at the foot of the staircase. 'Trina, wouldn't you like me to come with you?' I asked as I helped her on with her coat.

'No, no, my child. You stay here with Sarah. Bella will wait up for us, and we'll have coffee when we get back.'

Johan entered from the court-yard. He wore his coat with the collar turned up, and both the lanterns were lit. He gave one to Trina and firmly took her arm. The north-west gale whipped their coats about their legs, pushing and buffeting them as they left the shelter of the house. We watched until we could only see the two swaying lanterns in the dark.

We sat in silence by the fire, unable to read, listening to the howling wind and the rattling of the old sash windows. Chiang slept on my lap and I stroked him absentmindedly, waiting for the time to pass.

They were gone for two hours. Johan came in, alone. He'd taken off his coat and his wet hair clung to his forehead.

Sarah gave an inarticulate cry and ran across the

132

room, flinging herself into his arms. 'Oh, darling! Are you all right?'

His arms closed around her. 'Yes, I'm all right.'

She ran her fingers through his hair and pushed it off his forehead. 'You're wet.'

'It started to rain half an hour ago.' He looked at me over the top of her head. 'Anna, will you go to Ma. I think she needs you.'

I found her in the bathroom, huddled over the basin. She looked up as I entered. Her face was gaunt and grey and the sweat glistened on her forehead. I moistened a towel under the tap and gently wiped her brow. She took it and buried her face in it; then sank down on the stool, bowed and silent. Her body was twitching and she shivered uncontrollably.

I ran to her room and found her woollen dressing-gown. When I returned she stood up like a child, and let me wrap it around her. She sat down again, silently nodding her thanks, and briefly touched my cheek. 'Oh, Anna,' she whispered. 'I'm so glad I didn't let you come.' She swayed and moaned softly. 'If only our minds could be a slate – if only we could take a wet sponge and wipe out what we want to forget.' She shuddered. 'To be able to obliterate memories of what we've seen, heard – and smelled.' She rose quickly and clung to the edge of the basin, retching painfully.

Later I put my arm around her and leaning on me heavily, she walked to her room. She sat in the chair next to her bed and palely smiled at me. 'I feel old and tired, darling. I think I'll go to bed.'

'I'll fetch you a cup of coffee.'

She shuddered and grimaced. 'No, not coffee! You know what you can do, darling? Go to the dining-room and if you look in the right-hand corner cupboard you'll find a bottle of K.W.V. brandy – bring it up with two brandy balloons. 'No wait!' she cried as I reached the door. 'I've just remembered that James gave Johannes a bottle of Remy Martin for Christmas – bring that instead. And, Anna!' she called a second later. 'See you can persuade Johannes to have a glass of cognac – it will do him good.'

I found the bottle of Remy Martin at the back of the corner cupboard and placed it on a silver tray with four brandy goblets, then carried it through to the sitting-room. Johan was sitting in front of the fire, his hands clasped between his knees and glanced up as I entered.

'You look tired, Johan. Trina said I must persuade you to have a little cognac.'

He smiled. 'That's a good idea.'

I put the tray on the slate-topped table and poured the brandy into a goblet, handing it to him. 'Where's Sarah?' I asked.

'She's gone to bed. I'm waiting for the police. I rang them half an hour ago.'

He glanced up as I reached for the tray. 'Pour a brandy for yourself,' he said quietly, 'and sit with me for a few minutes.'

I sank into the chair opposite him, clasping the glass between my hands, staring into its fiery depths. We sat in silence – the only sound in the room the crackling of the fire.

I glanced up and saw him looking at me intently. He lifted his glass, sipped the brandy and cupped it again between his hands. 'How's Ma?'

'Oh, Johan, I've never seen her like this! She seems broken.' I half rose. 'I must go to her.'

'Wait a bit longer. She won't mind. I'm glad you were here, Anna – you can help her more than anyone. She'll be all right tomorrow morning – you'll see. I've always told you, Ma's an indomitable woman.' He

134

looked at me. 'Your head isn't aching tonight,' he said gently.

Instinctively I put my hand to the base of my skull. 'How did you know?'

'I always know when you have a headache,' he said quietly.

The door opened and Sarah came in. She was wearing a long ruby-red robe and her silky black hair was clubbed back. 'What are you two doing in here?' She walked over to the fireplace and stood between us. 'I thought you were with Trina,' she said coldly.

'I was. She sent me down for a bottle of Remy Martin and asked me to persuade Johan to have some.' I jumped up. 'Won't you have some too?'

'No!' she said rudely. She looked at Johan. 'When are you coming up?'

He continued staring into his glass. 'I told you, I'm waiting for the police. Why don't you go to bed?'

'No, I'll stay with you until they come.' She looked at me pointedly. 'Don't let us keep you.'

'I'm going.' I picked up the tray. 'Trina will be wondering where I am.'

She was sitting in bed smoking a cigarette, wrapped in a red woollen bed-jacket. Her hair was combed and there was a faint touch of colour in her cheeks. Her face had lost the greyish pallor which had frightened me so much.

'Did you persuade Johannes to have a little brandy?'

'Yes.'

'I'm glad – it will help him to relax. Poor Johannes,' she sighed.

I poured out a brandy and she took the glass from me, lifting it to her nose and sniffing it delicately. She placed a pillow behind her head and leaned back, looking at me over the rim of her glass.

'What a sad and dreadful business this has been. I can't forget those poor children. Adonis set Annekie alight in front of them. They saw and heard everything! That poor child tried to run out of the house when she was burning and fell and died on the threshold of her home.' She swirled the brandy in her glass. 'Those unfortunate children are virtually orphans now. I'll have to find out if Annekie's mother and sister who live in Paarl will be prepared to take them in.'

'Was he there when you and Johan arrived?'

'Who, darling?'

'Adonis.' I could hardly bring myself to say his name.

'No. Nobody thought of apprehending him. You know how emotional and excitable the *volk* are. They were so upset and stunned that they forgot about him.'

'He'll hang for this!'

'Not necessarily. He was drunk at the time.'

'Surely that's no excuse!' I cried indignantly. 'Everyone knows how brutally he's treated her.'

'If it could be proved that Adonis was drunk,' she said quietly, 'I doubt if, legally, they could hang him.' She paused, frowning slightly and changed the subject. 'I'm worried about Johannes. He's been so quiet lately – he's not himself. Things haven't been the same between him and Adonis since that day Johannes hit him. I know he'll reproach himself unnecessarily.'

'He can't possibly blame himself for what's happened.'

'Johannes will. I know my son.' She handed the goblet to me. 'Pour me another brandy, Anna.' When I gave it to her, she held it under her nose, savouring the bouquet. 'Johannes has changed. I hoped the week he spent with Sarah in Johannesburg would do him good – but he's more silent than ever.' She paused. 'He told me he'd 'phone the police tonight.'

136

'He's already done so.'

'They'll find Adonis of course, wherever he's hiding. The *volk* are now solidly against him and will do all they can to help.'

But the police didn't find him. Reports were received that Adonis had been seen in Worcester, Ceres and Beaufort West – even as far afield as Port Elizabeth. On investigation these rumours proved groundless. He had vanished completely.

The entire coloured community of Wonderkloof and Mooi Vlei, dressed in their Sunday best, turned out for Annekie's funeral. There wasn't a dry eye amongst them during the service. Annekie's four children, wide-eyed and bewildered, stood in a group near the grave with her old mother, who held the baby. After the funeral she shook hands with Trina and Johan and took the baby and children with her.

When Trina and I entered the kitchen the next morning, I heard Bella talking to Lettie.

She stopped and turned around, smiling unctuously. 'Good-morning, *Merrem*. Good-morning, Miss Anna.' She folded her arms and kept the smile on her face. 'I jes telling Lettie, *Merrem*, that Gawd now punish her for what she done to her mother.' She turned and looked at Lettie. 'The child what she bear is the child of a dirty murderer!' Lettie shrank as though flayed by a whip and Bella's small mean eyes lit with triumph. 'Yes, a murderer!' she shouted. 'And the child will be a murderer, jes like his father! Now you bring shame on yourself jes like you bring shame on your mother – you dirty slut!'

'Leave the child alone!' Trina cried angrily.

But Bella had found the weapon she had been searching for. Day after day we heard the steady drone of her loud sanctimonious voice coming from the kitchen; and

Lettie crept about the house, a figure of shame, never lifting her eyes.

Adonis became the bogey man of the district. His name was used to frighten young girls and terrify little children.

Chapter Nineteen

I SAW LITTLE of Sarah during the first three months she lived at Wonderkloof. She came down every morning and had breakfast with us, leaving the dining-room with Johan when the meal was over. If the weather was fine she often remained with him all morning, sketching or doing impressionistic paintings of the countryside. Two or three times a week she drove to Cape Town in her dark blue Mercedes 300 SL coupé to shop or visit her dressmaker. Her cupboards were filled with glamorous elegant clothes, not always suited to the quiet life she lived at Wonderkloof. She and Johan sometimes went out at night and it was on these occasions that Trina and I admired her sophisticated and lavish wardrobe.

'Sarah's paintings are remarkably good,' Trina said.

It was a sunny day and we were in the garden pruning the roses. She was wearing thick pruning gloves, a chestnut-brown gardening smock and a large straw hat.

'At least there's one thing we can thank Johannes' grandfather for,' she said, kneeling and cutting out a piece of dead wood. 'We've an excellent collection of pictures at Wonderkloof, due to the great interest that old roué took in the work of our South African artists. On the whole he chose well – most of the pictures we have are good examples of their work.' She looked at me. 'Did you know that Pieter Wenning, our most famous South African artist, once stayed a week at Wonderkloof? This was before he became famous. Johannes' grandfather found him painting on the side of the road and stopped to look at his work. He was so impressed that he invited Wenning to stay. During that time he painted the two pictures which are in the sitting-room. They cost Johannes' grandfather thirty-nine pounds for the two – today they're worth thousands.' She smiled. 'Wenning told Johannes' grandmother that when he made preparations to set out on a painting trip, his wife gave him a batch of post-cards, stamped and addressed. On each one she wrote "I am well." During his trip, when he remembered, he posted one to her.'

She waved her secateurs. 'Attie!' she called loudly. 'Come here and cut out this piece of dead wood. I can't manage it.'

He put down his spade, muttering inaudibly under his breath and unsmilingly shambled over to us. She handed the secateurs to him and watched critically while he removed the dead branch.

'See that you burn it – and all the other branches. I don't want any rose cuttings thrown on the compost heap.' She straightened and rubbed the small of her back. 'Attie!' she called again. 'Miss Anna and I will finish the pruning by tonight. If there's no wind tomorrow morning I want the roses sprayed. Then you and Christiaan must spread manure on the beds.' He nodded without speaking and she turned back to me. 'As I was saying, Sarah's very talented. The oil she did of the wine-cellar is excellent. I'm having it framed and shall put it in Johannes' study. The labels she designed for the Wonderkloof wines are quite outstanding.' She sighed. 'I only wish she'd spend more time at home instead of gallivanting in Cape Town buying clothes. I'm not happy about the child driving such a fast car – though Johannes assures me she's a careful driver. One of these days she'll have to settle down and take an interest in the garden and the running of the house.'

She threw the secateurs into the gardening basket and stripped off her gloves. 'Come, my child, let's go and have a cup of tea. I told Sannie to put the tea tray in Johannes' study at eleven o'clock. I'm thirsty and would also like a cigarette.' She took my arm. 'Did I tell you that Bettie has offered to take Lettie into one of the coloured cottages at Mooi Vlei? She has a decent old washerwoman called Mabel, who lives with her widowed daughter. They've agreed to take Lettie in and look after her. I've arranged with the District Nurse to keep an eye on her and help her when the baby's born. As you know, Christina was going to look after her, but I've discovered that she's under Bella's influence. Last week I overheard her searing at the poor child. Tomorrow we'll take her to Mooi Vlei. Sannie and Hettie will take her place – Bella, of course, will bully them unmercifully.'

The next morning there was no wind and Trina spent half an hour supervising the spraying of the rose trees. 'Attie! See you don't dawdle while I'm gone, I'll expect you to be finished when I get back.'

Lettie sat in the back of the car answering only in monosyllables when we spoke to her.

Tant' Bettie saw us drive up the avenue and met us in front of the house. '*Ag*, Trina, isn't it a lovely day!' She kissed me and turned to Lettie, smiling kindly. 'Go to the kitchen, child. Cookie will give you a cup of tea and Mabel will be here in half an hour to fetch you.'

Lettie picked up her suitcase and trudged to the kitchen door without looking at us.

'Lettie,' Trina called. 'Miss Anna and I will come and

see you. You've everything you need and Mabel and her daughter will look after you. Now you've nothing to worry about.' Lettie didn't answer her or look back.

The almond blossom and fat pink buds on the magnolia tree heralded the approach of spring.

Colonel Jamieson's return to South Africa coincided with the arrival of the first swallows at Wonderkloof. Swooping through the casement windows of the upper hall, a pair returned to their nest in the corner of the passage leading to my bedroom. One evening the Colonel strode unannounced into the sitting-room, looking tanned and well.

'Good heavens, James!' Trina exclaimed. 'I didn't expect you back before the middle of the month.'

'My dearest Trina.' He put his arm around her and kissed her. 'How well you're looking – and how I've missed you!'

She smiled. 'And how nice to have you back, James.'

'I've dinner organized and a bottle of champagne on ice – will you dine with me?'

She moved away and patted her hair. 'Yes, thank you, but I must have half an hour to change.'

'My dear, you look charming as you are!'

'No, I insist on changing,' she set her lips firmly. 'You relax in front of the fire with Anna and I'll send Sannie in with the drink tray.'

He crossed the room and shook my hand. 'Good-evening, my dear Anna.' He stood back and looked at me searchingly. 'You're much better. When you and Trina were in London, I thought you looked wretchedly ill.'

'I was suffering from bad headaches at the time,' I said shyly.

'Oh, I'm so sorry to hear that. I trust they've

142

improved now that you're once again enjoying the bracing air of Wonderkloof.' He waited for me to be seated. 'Did Trina tell you that I went to Bermuda and finished my book there?'

'Yes.'

'I needed sun and peace, and found both. I hope, my dear Anna, that I'll be able to persuade you to type my new book.'

'Certainly. I'll do it with pleasure.'

'Good! Excellent! I'm absolutely delighted! I must do a little revising – but hope to let you have it by the end of the week.'

He stood up as Johan and Sarah came in and grasped Johan's arm, shaking him firmly by the hand. 'Allow me to congratulate you, my dear Johan.' Looking admiringly at Sarah he gave a courtly bow. 'Not only on your marriage, dear boy, but also on the beauty of your wife! You're lovely, my child.'

'Thank you,' she murmured huskily.

Johan walked over to the table and lifted a glass. 'What will you have, Sir?'

'A whiskey and soda would be delightful, dear boy.'

Half an hour later, Trina found us in front of the fire listening to Colonel Jamieson's vivid and sometimes lurid descriptions of life in Bermuda.

He went to her and put his arm around her waist. 'I've been telling Johan and Sarah that they should spend a holiday in Bermuda.'

'Don't be ridiculous!' she said brusquely. 'Johannes has neither the time nor money to spend gallivanting around Bermuda.' She tapped his arm. 'Before I forget, James. Will you dine with us on Saturday – three weeks from today?'

'I'd be delighted, my dear.'

'Gert and Bettie will be coming, and Mrs Fourie and

her son are spending the weekend with us.' She looked at Johan. 'D'you remember them, Johannes?'

'Vaguely, Ma.'

'You must remember them!' she said impatiently. 'You've met him – that rather dark young man from Swellendam – I think he played rugby for their first team. He lives with his mother.'

'Oh, d'you mean Ben Fourie?'

'That's right – I thought he was a charming boy.'

He cast a glance in my direction. 'Yes, Ma,' he said dryly.

'Good-night, children. Don't wait up for me. I'll see you at breakfast tomorrow morning.' She swept out on Colonel Jamieson's arm.

I quickly turned to Johan. 'What's he like?'

'Who?' he asked innocently.

'You know whom, Johan. Don't pretend you don't! This Ben Fourie or whatever his name is, from Swellendam?'

'Oh, Ben!' He looked up at the ceiling while I waited impatiently, then grinned wickedly. 'He's a damned pompous bore!' he said succinctly.

'I knew it!' I groaned. 'I knew it! If only Maria were here I'd stay with her at Mooi Vlei.'

'You wouldn't have a hope! Ma wouldn't permit it. She'll expect you to take Ben for long walks.'

I was irritated by his smile. 'I won't do it!' I cried.

'As you know, Ma's a great organizer. You and Ben will be thrown into each other's company and practically into each other's arms, morning, noon and night. Everything will be arranged from the moment you open your eyes in the morning.'

'You didn't find it so funny when she tried to organize you.'

'Ma, my dear Anna, is an indefatigable matchmaker.' He burst out laughing.

'Why are you laughing?' I asked sourly. Then, against my will, I smiled.

'What's amusing you two so much?' Sarah asked coldly. She was looking at us without a trace of a smile.

'It's Ma. She's a tireless matchmaker. For years she's invited the dullest girls imaginable to spend weekends at Wonderkloof hoping to marry me off to one of them.' He grinned. 'Now she's started on Anna who's enjoying it no more than I did.'

'I'm surprised you're not more sympathetic,' I grumbled.

'Actually,' Sarah drawled, looking at me coolly, 'I'm surprised you haven't thought of settling down.'

'What exactly d'you mean by settling down?' I asked, equally coldly.

'It's quite obvious what I mean. Don't you intend getting married sometime?'

I tried to smile despite my annoyance. 'There's plenty of time for me to think about it – I'll only be twenty-two next month. I suppose I'll marry eventually when I meet the right man.'

'In spite of what Johan says, this Ben Fourie may be the right man.'

'I very much doubt it,' I said stonily.

'Johan, why did you try to prejudice Anna against him?' She was looking at him with pale intensity. 'Why did you put her off before she's even met him?'

'Good Lord.' His smile was tight-lipped. 'I couldn't imagine that my opinion of Ben would influence Anna one way or the other.'

'It *has* influenced her!' She turned and looked at me again. 'What about Martin Joubert?'

'What about him?'

145

'He seemed quite interested in you.'

'Did he?' I said icily.

'Yes, he did! Perhaps he'll marry you.'

'Well I'm not the slightest bit interested in him!' I cried, no longer able to control my temper. 'Nor am I interested in marrying anyone else!'

'How extraordinary. What could be your reason?'

'Sarah!' I cried angrily. 'Will you kindly mind your own damned business!'

She gave a closed little smile. 'That's where you're wrong, Anna. It is my business. I'm married to Johan and Wonderkloof happens to be my home.'

'What on earth are you talking about? What d'you mean?'

'My meaning should be quite clear. Surely you don't intend living at Wonderkloof indefinitely?'

I recoiled as though she'd struck me. 'No, Sarah,' I said rather breathlessly, with as much dignity as I could summon. 'It isn't my intention to live at Wonderkloof indefinitely. I haven't given much thought to the future. At the moment, however, I regard Wonderkloof as my home – I probably love it as much as you do.'

The corner of her mouth lifted in an unattractive smile. 'That's beside the point. The truth of the matter is, this isn't your home, is it?'

Before I could reply, Johan hastily interrupted. 'Look at Chiang!' He was lying on his back in front of the fire between Wolf's forepaws, with his legs in the air and his eyes closed. Johan knelt and stroked him. 'He's doubled his size in the last six months and has his full winter coat. D'you remember how small he was when I gave him to you, Anna?' Though he looked up he avoided my eyes.

'You never told me you gave Chiang to her.' It was almost a whisper.

'Didn't I?' His expression was strangely wary. He fondled Chiang's ears, then got up and sat on the sofa.

'Why didn't you tell me?'

'I thought you knew.'

'You know perfectly well that isn't true! Why didn't you tell me?' she repeated, her voice rising.

'Because I didn't think it was of the slightest importance.' Though he sounded bored his eyes narrowed and his face paled.

'It *is* important! Why did you give Chiang to her? Answer me, Johan!'

'Sarah, for God's sake stop being so damned ridiculous!' he exploded angrily.

'Don't you dare shout at me!' Her eyes were blazing. 'I'm asking you for the last time – why did you give Chiang to her?'

'Chiang was a birthday present,' I said quickly. 'Trina gave me a typewriter, Pieter a bottle of perfume – and Johan gave Chiang to me. It was shortly after my mother died and I was lonely and unhappy – it was a wonderful present. He has given me companionship and happiness.'

She didn't look at me; she moved over to the fireplace and stared down at the two dogs. Then her face froze and she viciously kicked Chiang. 'I hate pekinese!' she said in a low vibrant voice.

Chapter Twenty

FROM THAT NIGHT my life at Wonderkloof was never the same. It marked the beginning of a nightmare which would darken each day and cast a shadow on my spirit, almost quenching it. It was also the birth of my dislike for Sarah which would blossom into an obsessive bitter hatred.

The next evening we were grouped round the fire in the sitting-room. Trina and I were reading and Johan sat on the sofa looking at the evening paper. Sarah was doing a rough sketch of Wolf who lay curled on the carpet in front of the fire.

'Why's Wolf such an unfriendly dog? Why doesn't he allow me to touch him?'

Johan glanced up from his paper. 'He's a one man dog.'

Trina removed her spectacles. 'I've always said, Johannes – what's the use of having an animal that likes only one person in the house? Look at Chiang, we know he loves Anna most, yet he's friendly with the rest of us.'

'Chiang's different,' I said. 'He has a warm affectionate nature. Wolf's the Spitz breed with a withdrawn character.'

'I don't agree with you,' Sarah looked at me distantly.

'I don't think that's got anything to do with it! Everybody's assumed he's a one man dog just because Johan says so. I'm quite certain that I could make him like me.'

She dropped her sketch book next to her chair, walked over to the fireplace and looked down at Wolf. Instinct told him that her attention was fixed on him. He opened his eyes and lifted his head; as she bent to stroke him he leapt to his feet and shied away, padding silently across the room to stop in front of my chair. Keeping his dark brown, intelligent eyes fixed on mine, he sniffed at Chiang. I hardly dared breathe; then hesitantly I stretched out my hand and gently placed it on his head. He remained still, keeping his eyes on me. I curved my fingers and caressed him behind the ears. He allowed his muzzle to sink on to Chiang's back and I felt him relax and move closer.

'Well I'll be damned!' Johan said softly.

'Johannes, there'll be no swearing in this house!' Trina said automatically; but she smiled.

I continued to caress Wolf's ears, absurdly moved. Glancing up, I saw Sarah staring at me with an expression of such undisguised hatred that my stomach contracted. 'It's – it's only because of Chiang,' I stammered. 'He hasn't taken the slightest notice of me before.'

She turned away and ripped the page out of her sketch book and with one fierce gesture tore it in half and threw it in the fire.

Trina rose abruptly. 'Come, children. I heard the bell. We're starting with a cheese soufflé and mustn't be late.' She took my arm as we walked through the hall. 'I forgot to tell you – Bettie 'phoned this afternoon to say that Lettie's had a daughter. We certainly got her to Mooi Vlei in the nick of time! I asked Bettie to tell her that we'll see the baby tomorrow morning.' She shook her head and lowered her voice. 'When I went into the kitchen to tell Bella the news, she didn't say a word – just sniffed and went on working.'

'Can I take you to Mooi Vlei tomorrow, Trina?' Sarah said as we entered the dining-room.

'Oh,' Trina said doubtfully.

Johan laughed as he drew out her chair. 'You'll be safe, Ma. She's a careful driver.'

'I've no doubt, but Sarah has a two-seater and there wouldn't be room for all of us. Where would Anna sit?'

'Oh.' Sarah lifted her eyebrows, and sat down unfolding her napkin. 'Does she want to come?'

'Don't worry about me,' I said quickly. 'I'm quite happy to stay at home.'

'Nonsense!' Trina said firmly. 'Of course you must come. We'll go in my car and you can drive, Anna.'

'But you'll let me take you for a drive one day, won't you?' Sarah smiled at her rather fixedly.

'Of course, my dear. I'd enjoy it.'

She turned as Sannie handed her the dish and plunged the spoon into the fluffy golden-brown soufflé.

'And tomorrow,' Sarah continued huskily, still smiling at Trina, 'I want to start helping you in the house and garden. I feel so ashamed I've done nothing since coming to live here.'

Trina reached across and gripped her hand impulsively. 'I'm delighted, Sarah! Only the other day I said to Anna that it's time you started. After all, this is your home and you must learn to run this big old house.'

'That's exactly what I told her,' Sarah said, transferring her smile to me.

'By the way,' Johan said, energetically grinding the pepper mill and looking at me across the table. 'There're a few details I'd like to discuss with you. That account from Reedeman's, for instance – haven't they overcharged us?'

'No, I thought so too, but when I 'phoned to check, they explained that fertilizer's gone up.'

'Everything goes up!' Trina exclaimed angrily. 'I don't know how the poor farmers are expected to make a living.'

'That's another thing.' Sarah looked at Trina intensely. 'Don't you think I should help Johan with the accounts? As you've said – I'll live here all my life and should know about the running of the farm.'

Trina smiled at her kindly. 'All in good time, my dear. At the moment I think we should leave that department to Anna. She has the training and handles the business side extremely well.'

Sarah's face paled. 'I'd do it just as well! I'll take a course in book-keeping and typing.' Her jaw set obstinately. 'I *want* to do the accounts with Johan!'

He was sipping his wine and looked at her as he put his glass on the table with a sharp click. 'That's out of the question,' he said flatly. 'Anna must do them. She's efficient and we're damned lucky to have her!' For once Trina didn't reprimand him for swearing.

The blood rose to my cheeks – at last I'd received my word of praise.

The following morning we had tea with *Tant'* Bettie at Mooi Vlei. She always had morning tea at the round dining-room table. There were *soet Koekies*, a batch of hot scones, golden farm butter, a bowl of thick cream, watermelon *konfyt*, and home-made strawberry jam.

Tant' Bettie was friendly and polite when she greeted Sarah, but I noticed again that she did not kiss her.

'We can't stay too long, Bettie,' Trina said. 'I want Sarah and Anna to help me wash the porcelain and glass

151

which I don't allow the servants to touch on any account – you know how careless they are. I told Bella to see that Sannie and Hettie put basins of warm water in the hall and sitting-room by a quarter to twelve, so we must be back by then.'

Tant' Bettie sighed. 'How lucky you are to have the girls to help you. This old house is so quiet and empty with both my children gone.'

'When d'you expect Julian back?' Trina asked evenly.

'I had a letter from him yesterday. He's returning at the end of the month. There's lots of work to do on the farm and Gert needs him.' She pushed her chair back. 'If you want to be back at a quarter to twelve we should go and see Lettie at once.' She put her arm around my waist. 'I had a letter from Maria today. She seems to be a good cook and makes fancy dishes I've never heard of. She even sends me the recipes! I smile when I think how we quarrelled when I tried to teach her how to cook. She sends her love and will be writing to you next week.'

Mabel's flat-roofed white-washed cottage stood a hundred yards from the homestead under a spreading oak. Inside it smelled of woodsmoke, but the walls were white-washed and it was tidy and spotlessly clean. The frilled floral curtains were freshly laundered and the table in the centre of the tiny living-room was covered with a cloth embroidered with flowers.

Tant' Bettie held up a corner of the cloth. 'Look at this!' Trina put on her spectacles and examined the needlework closely. 'Mabel did this. I bought the cloth and gave it to her for Christmas. Look how beautifully she's embroidered it.'

Families of up to eight or ten crowded into the coloured cottages at Mooi Vlei and Wonderkloof, eating, sleeping and living together; the children witnessing their parents' quarrels, drunkenness and lovemaking.

In this cottage, Mabel shared a bedroom with her daughter, and Lettie had a room to herself. She was alone in the house, and was sitting up in bed cradling the baby and smiled as we entered.

Motherhood had improved her. Her face was soft and happy. The baby was light-skinned like her mother and father and her tiny face was old and wizened like a monkey's.

'What a beautiful baby, Lettie!' Trina exclaimed, reaching down and taking the baby from her. Cradling the infant in her arms, she gently stroked her cheek. 'Her skin's like silk.'

'She beautiful, *Ou Nooi*. One day she the prettiest coloured girl at Wonderkloof.'

'What are you going to call her?'

'I call her Wiolet, *Ou Nooi*,' she smiled shyly. 'Because she look like a little flower.' She glanced at me. 'Miss Anna, will Miss Anna be Wiolet's godmother?'

'Me!' I exclaimed. 'You want me to be Violet's godmother?' Sarah stirred beside me.

'Yes, Miss Anna.'

'Thank you, Lettie. I'd love to be her godmother. I'll buy her a christening mug next time I'm in Cape Town.'

Driving back to Wonderkloof, I took my eye off the road to look at Trina. 'I'm very touched that Lettie's asked me to be Violet's godmother. I was so taken aback that I must have appeared ungracious. I honestly don't know why she asked me. She's never particularly liked me.'

Trina laughed and patted my knee. 'Keep your eye on the road, Anna! I know why Lettie asked you. The coloured people are like children – they're infallible judges of character. Lettie knows that you're good and kind.' She looked over her shoulder. 'Don't you agree, Sarah? Don't you think the coloured people are excellent judges of character?'

There was a long pause. 'I've no idea.' Her voice was icy. 'We've only Bantu servants in Johannesburg.'

We found two enamel basins filled with water placed on the floor next to the court-yard windows, and a neat pile of drying cloths stacked on a chair.

'Come, children,' Trina said briskly. 'We must hurry if we want to be finished before lunch.' She dipped her finger in the water. 'It's just cool enough.' She added a dash of detergent. 'Now, when we've collected the china and glass, I want it to be washed in the warm water and rinsed in the cold – and for goodness sake, be careful! I shouldn't really have these pieces on the tables, but as long as the servants don't dust them they're reasonably safe. I can't bring myself to lock them away – many are museum pieces. Take this heart-shaped toilet box, for instance.' She showed us the dark-blue china box. 'This was brought to Wonderkloof by Johannes' great-grandmother, Gertrude Barton. Look at the lamb and the fat little cupids – it dates from about 1760 and was made in Chelsea. I believe there's one almost identical to it in the British Museum. Gertrude Barton had a weakness for dark-blue porcelain – she bought the two blue and gold Sèvres vases in the sitting-room. Some of the glass and china, of course, has only sentimental value, but they're all irreplaceable.'

We collected and placed the pieces near the enamel basins.

'Now squat on the floor and sit on those cushions. You're both young enough to sit like that – and for goodness sake be careful! Concentrate on what you're doing and don't talk too much! I'll leave you now and wash the things in the sitting-room.'

The moment she left Sarah turned to me. 'How long d'you intend living here?'

I looked up from the milkmaid I was dipping in the water. 'What have you against me, Sarah? Why d'you dislike me so much?'

'I don't dislike you,' her expression was aloof. 'I just want to know how long you intend to live here.'

'I'll live here as long as Trina wishes me to stay.' My voice trembled.

'What has Trina got to do with it? This is Johan's home and mine – we've the right to live in it alone!'

'This is also Trina's home. She's lived here most of her life. What about Trina, Sarah? What are your plans for her?'

'We're not discussing Trina. We're discussing you.'

'But what are your plans for her?' I persisted. 'Will you allow her to live with you and Johan?'

She picked up a black and gold Bohemian vase and dipped it in the water. 'She'll probably marry Colonel Jamieson.'

I smiled. 'I wouldn't bank on that! I don't think she has the slightest intention of marrying Colonel Jamieson, or anyone else for that matter. If you don't believe me, ask Johan.'

'I won't ask Johan, and we're not discussing Trina!' She put the glass vase on the floor and looked at me with an unpleasant sneer. 'I must say, you've a thick hide to continue living in a house where you're not wanted.'

My hands were shaking. I carefully removed the lid of the little heart-shaped toilet box. 'Trina wants me to stay here.'

'Well, I don't! This is my house and I dislike having strangers living in it.'

'I'm hardly a stranger. Trina's known me all my life.'

'Well, I haven't! You're not a member of the family. What makes you think you've the right to inflict yourself on us?'

I looked at her levelly. 'Sarah, I'll leave Wonderkloof when Trina or Johan tell me to go, not before.'

Her eyes blazed and she struck my arm. The lid of the toilet box flew out of my hand and smashed to the floor.

Trina came dashing through the sitting-room door, her eyes wide with consternation. 'What's happened? I heard something break! What was it?' Her eyes fell on the broken lid lying at my feet. 'Oh, no!' She knelt and picked up the pieces with her slim brown fingers. She looked as though she were about to cry and her eyes flashed. 'How could you be so careless, Anna!'

'I'm sorry,' I mumbled. I looked at Sarah, but she kept her head down.

'Saying sorry isn't going to mend it! I should never have let you touch these treasures. In future, I'll do them myself.'

'Oh, please let me help you,' Sarah pleaded. 'I promise I'll be very careful. These will one day belong to Johan and me and I love every piece as much as you do.'

I flung the drying cloth on the floor, jumped up and ran out of the room.

Chapter Twenty-one

THAT WEEK SARAH started her campaign in earnest. She no longer walked with Johan after breakfast, but accompanied us to the kitchen, where she had animated conversations with Bella and Trina while I stood silently by. They were fired by her determination to learn everything; Bella beamingly answered her questions, swelling with pride and importance.

'I always said Sarah would be a capable girl,' Trina remarked. 'I hope that she and Johannes will hurry up and start a family.'

Sarah showed the same enthusiasm in the garden, questioning *Ou* Attie and *Ou* Christiaan and working tirelessly at Trina's side. Though I admired the zeal and energy with which she tackled each task, feeling it only right that she should play an active part in the running of Wonderkloof, I was unable to forgive her for the veiled sneers directed at me when we were alone, the slights and secret looks like the thrust of a dagger, and her cruelty to Chiang.

The first time she trod on him I thought it was accidental; but when it happened repeatedly and unnecessarily, I knew it was deliberate.

'Be careful, Sarah! Surely you could see Chiang was lying next to my chair.'

'If I'd seen him I obviously wouldn't have trodden on him!'

'Please be careful in future.'

'If you don't want me to tread on that animal, keep him out of my way.'

If she found me alone in the sitting-room and saw Chiang sleeping on a chair she'd seize him by the scruff of his neck and fling him on the floor.

'Don't do that, Sarah!'

'If you don't want me to do it, keep that dog off the furniture.'

'Leave him alone! No one else objects to him lying there.'

'I object, and it's my house.'

Whenever Johan and Trina were present she was hypocritically charming. Plying me with questions and talking animatedly to me. I met her advances with chilliness and silence.

My behaviour worried Trina and she became fidgety and looked at me repeatedly when I ignored Sarah's advances. I glanced up once and saw Johan looking at me oddly.

At breakfast a few days later, Trina was called to the telephone. 'That was Bettie,' she said when she returned. 'She says Lettie's vanished.'

'Vanished!'

'Yes. Mabel and her daughter apparently visited friends: when they returned they found that Lettie and the baby had disappeared. None of the *volk* saw her leave. How could she manage to carry the baby and all her things? I can't think what's happened to her – I'm so worried about the poor child.'

'D'you think she's gone off with Adonis?' I asked.

'No. I'd think that's extremely unlikely,' she said impatiently. 'Adonis is a fugitive from justice and hardly likely to saddle himself with a woman and baby.' She pushed her chair back. 'Come, children, you've finished. I must tell Bella what's happened.'

Bella was kneading bread at the kitchen table.

Trina came directly to the point. 'Bella, I've just had a 'phone call from Madam Retief at Mooi Vlei. She tells me that Lettie and the baby have disappeared.'

Bella pursed her lips and looked at Trina in silence, then hitched up her sleeves and went on kneading.

'Bella, did you hear what I said?'

'Yes, *Merrem*,' she said heavily. 'I hear.'

'Then why don't you answer me? Have you any idea what could have happened to them?'

'No, *Merrem*.'

'Are there any relatives or friends she might have gone to visit?'

'No, *Merrem*.'

'Aren't you worried about the poor child?'

Bella looked up, her black face impassive. 'Lettie no concern of mine.'

'How can you say that! She's your child – you must be concerned about her!'

Bella lifted the dough out of the basin. 'Where Lettie's gorn isn't my business. She must look after herself.'

'Is that all you have to say!' Trina looked at her angrily. Bella put the dough in the bread tins. 'You're a hard woman, Bella – and an unnatural mother!' She turned and walked quickly out of the kitchen. Sarah and I followed her into the hall. 'If we hear nothing by this evening I'll have to 'phone the police.'

She was ahead of us and Sarah was next to me. She suddenly pushed me so that I staggered sideways and fell against the gueridon. I saw the Imari vase topple over and tried desperately to save it – my fingers just

159

touched it before it crashed to the floor and shattered into a thousand fragments.

'Anna!' Trina cried, her face white with shock. 'You've broken the Imari vase!' Her hand was clutched over her heart.

I looked at Sarah. 'You pushed me!'

She was next to Trina. 'What are you talking about? I wasn't near you!'

'You pushed me!' I repeated slowly.

Her eyes filled with tears and she put her hand to her face. 'You know perfectly well that isn't true. How can you make such an accusation!' She burst into tears. 'She knows I didn't push her,' she sobbed. 'Why should I do such a thing? Why doesn't Anna like me, Trina? What have I done?'

Trina's face was pale. 'Don't cry, my child.' She looked at me with haunted eyes. 'What's come over you, darling? Why are you behaving like this?'

I looked at her steadily; then I turned and walked out of the room.

From that day I didn't accompany Trina and Sarah to the kitchen, nor did I work with them in the garden.

'Come, children,' Trina would say after breakfast, looking at me, not Sarah. 'Let's go.'

'I can't come with you this morning – I've too much work and I'm behind with Colonel Jamieson's book.'

'Do come, darling,' she pleaded. 'You could do your typing later.'

'No, Trina.'

My bitterness included Trina – I was unable to forgive her for doubting me. When I rudely ignored Sarah's advances and saw Trina looking at me unhappily, I coolly returned her look. As soon as Sarah entered the room, I pointedly picked up Chiang and put him on my

160

lap, rejoicing at Trina's fidgeting and discomfort when I did so.

One morning when I got up from the breakfast table, Trina quickly caught my arm and squeezed me affectionately. 'No, Anna. I'm not going to let you run away this morning!'

'I must do the accounts,' I said stiffly.

'Do them later, darling,' she said with such a loving smile that the tears stung my eyes. Arm in arm we marched into the kitchen with Sarah trailing behind us.

Bella was beating butter and sugar in a striped blue bowl and rose as we entered. 'Good-morning, *Merrem*. Good-morning, Miss Anna.' She looked at me and smiled kindly, a hint of moisture in her eyes. 'I jes telling *Merrem* yesterday that I never see you no more, Miss Anna. Now I make the Madeira cake what you like.'

She knows! I thought. With the infallible instinct and shameless eavesdropping of the coloured servant, she, and probably Sannie and Hettie, knew what Sarah was doing – but they would never tell Trina.

'You see, darling!' Trina cried, squeezing my arm. 'You see how much we all miss you when you're not with us.'

Bella cleared her throat. 'Oh, *Merrem*. Last night I hear from my Lettie.'

'You've what! You've heard from Lettie! Where is she, Bella? Is she well?'

'Yes, *Merrem*, she well. She now live in Paarl. *Merrem* remember the young carpenter what was going to merry my Lettie? Well, he come in a car and fetch her and the baby and take them to his home. His mother and father make big troubles, but he say if he can't have my Lettie, he go away and work somewhere else. He love her, *Merrem*. He know my Lettie's a good girl – he know it only Adonis what led my little love astray.'

'I'm delighted! How happy you must be.'

'Yes, I heppy, *Merrem*. On Sunday I go to Paarl to see my Lettie and little Wiolet.' She paused and looked at Trina expectantly. 'I must let them know, *Merrem*, what the plans is for the wedding. You remember, you promised the reception at Wonderkloof. You also promised the wedding-cake and invitations.'

'So I did,' Trina said faintly.

'If *Merrem* buy the fruit and nuts, I make the cake and ice it,' she said magnanimously. 'I tell Lettie she can't get married until April, when we won't be so busy – by then she be thin and her wedding-dress will fit her like a dream. And the reception, *Merrem*,' she continued. 'I think we have in the big packing-shed.'

'I'll leave all the arrangements to you, Bella.'

When we entered the hall Trina threw her head back and laughed infectiously. 'Well, children,' she said, drying her eyes, 'it's raining and I've letters to write. Anna, I know you want to do the accounts. What will you do with yourself, my child?' she asked Sarah.

'I've lots to do.'

An hour later Sarah came into Johan's study. I was engrossed at his desk and looked up to see her standing at the door staring at me.

'What d'you want?' I asked ungraciously.

'Why are you working in here and not in your room?'

'I always do the accounts in Johan's study.'

'Why? You can do them perfectly well in your room.'

'I prefer to do them here.'

'And I prefer you to do them in your room!'

'That's just too bad.' I picked up my pen. 'And now, get out and let me finish my work.'

162

'I won't! You must show me how you do your book-keeping,' she said with contemptuous insolence.

'I thought you were going to take a course in book-keeping and typing.'

'I've changed my mind. I've decided you must teach me.'

'Well, I've no intention of doing so!'

Her nostrils were pinched and her face white with rage. Chiang was sleeping in the chair next to the door and she lashed out at him, striking him across the face; then seized him by the scruff of his neck and flung him on the floor.

'I've told you before I won't have that filthy beast lying on my furniture!'

Chiang yelped and ran to me, his tail between his legs. I picked him up and pressed my face against him. Shaking with rage I walked over to her.

'Sarah,' I said softly, 'I advise you never to do that again!'

'I'll do exactly as I please!'

'I'm warning you. Don't touch him again.'

'You're warning me!' she sneered. 'Who're you to tell me what to do in my own house!'

'I don't care if it's your house or not. Don't lay a finger on him again.'

'As I've told you before – I'll do exactly as I please! How could you stop me?'

I was trembling and had difficulty enunciating my words. 'I'll hit you! Every time you hurt Chiang I'll hit you as hard as I can!'

She raised her brows and her lip lifted. 'Really?'

Keeping her eyes on mine, she struck him viciously across his vulnerable eyes. As he yelped I smacked her face resoundingly. She gave a piercing scream and covered her face with her hands.

Seconds later Trina flew into the room. 'What's happened!' she cried in alarm. 'Did one of you scream?'

'Anna hit me,' Sarah sobbed. The mark where I'd struck her was vividly imprinted on her cheek.

Trina's face was frozen. 'Why did you hit her, Anna?'

'I came to ask her if she'd show me how to keep the books. She was rude and horrible, Trina! And then suddenly hit me.' She clung to Trina, her shoulders shaking.

Trina looked old and forbidding. 'How could you, Anna!'

'She hit Chiang,' I muttered. Even to my ears the excuse sounded ridiculous.

'How could you do such a thing!' Trina's voice was hoarse and strained. 'There's no excuse you can possibly make to justify such an action. What's come over you? What's wrong with you, darling?'

'There's nothing wrong with me. I detest cruelty and dishonesty, that's all!' My legs were trembling uncontrollably and I went over to the desk and sat down. 'Will you both go! I'd like to finish my work.' Trina looked at me in silence; then put her arm around Sarah and led her from the room.

I was still holding Chiang and bowed my head, clasping him tightly. 'Oh, Chiang,' I whispered. 'What can I do — what can I do?'

That night I waited for Trina, knowing she'd come to me. Though I expected her, nevertheless when she tapped on my door my heart lurched and beat faster.

'How's the typing going, darling?'

'I haven't done much.'

She came and stood next to me and put her hand on my shoulder. A week ago I would have looked up and smiled at her. Now I remained rigid, staring in front of me.

She sighed and sat on the edge of my bed looking tired and strained. 'Anna, darling, don't you think you've allowed yourself to become too attached to Chiang? You know—'

'There's nothing unnatural about my affection for Chiang!' I interrupted harshly.

'Darling, I didn't say your affection for Chiang was unnatural.' She paused, seeking her words.

'You think I'm jealous of Sarah, don't you?'

She looked at me helplessly, her face aged and haggard.

'Don't you?' I repeated.

She moved restlessly. 'Darling, I only want to say this—'

'Well, I'm not jealous of her,' I interrupted again. 'I'm not jealous of her, Trina. I hate her! I hate her damned guts!'

Everything I did and everything I said, played into Sarah's hands.

Chapter Twenty-two

I HARDLY NOTICED the spring that year. I didn't see the tender green leaves or the blossom on the fruit trees. The previous year I had watched the approach of spring with painful joy – now, so heavy a pall had fallen over my spirits that I was only dimly aware that it had started.

'Johannes,' Trina said at breakfast a week later. 'I'm afraid you'll have to come with me to Johannesburg. I got a letter from my broker yesterday. There're several vital decisions we must make and papers to be signed.'

'Why don't you do it through the post, Ma?'

'No, the arrangements must be made in person.'

'When d'you want to go?'

'It seems urgent, so the sooner the better. I thought we might fly to Johannesburg on Wednesday morning. There shouldn't be any difficulty in booking seats. I'll ring up this morning and make the necessary arrangements. Anna and I have appointments with the dentist this afternoon and we'll collect the tickets afterwards. This will give us three full days in Johannesburg. I don't want to rush things and I also promised Bettie to look up Maria. It will be an opportunity for you and Sarah to see something of your friends.' She looked at me. 'I'd like you to come with us, Anna. I know Maria will be delighted to see you.'

'No, thanks. I'd rather not.'

'Why not, darling?'

'I promised to finish Colonel Jamieson's book by the end of next week. I'll never do it if I go away for three days.'

'James wouldn't mind in the least if you took a few days longer. Let me 'phone him.'

'No, please don't! I promised – and I don't like breaking my word.'

She frowned. 'I'm not happy about leaving you here.'

'Don't worry Trina,' Sarah said with charming warmth. 'I'll stay with Anna.'

'No!' I cried, unable to check myself. 'I don't want you to stay!' Johan glanced up at me.

'Please let me, Trina,' Sarah pleaded. 'I really don't want to go on this trip – and I know you'll be happier if there's someone staying with Anna.'

'What about your family?' Trina said doubtfully. 'Wouldn't you like to see your brother and your friends?'

'No, I'd rather stay with Anna.'

'And I'd rather be alone!' I cried rudely. I looked at her angrily. 'Don't stay on my account – I'd infinitely prefer to be alone and you know it!'

'Anna!' Trina cried.

I pushed my chair back. 'Will you please excuse me.'

Before we left for Cape Town that afternoon I put Chiang in my room. I tossed him on to my bed and he lay down looking at me resignedly as I closed the door.

Trina was unusually silent during the drive, and it was only when we reached the outskirts of the city that she spoke to me for the first time.

'It will be your birthday the weekend after next. I'm so glad Pieter will be here to enjoy it with you. I'm disappointed that you wouldn't allow me to have a dance for you – you're becoming very stubborn, Anna. I thought I'd have one in December to give our relatives and friends a chance of meeting Sarah.' She paused and lit a cigarette. 'Darling, you must try and get on with her: after all, she's Johannes' wife. I'm very unhappy when you're rude to her.' My grip tightened on the wheel. 'You must admit it's extremely unselfish of her to offer to stay at Wonderkloof and keep you company. Not only were you ungrateful – I thought you were downright rude.'

'I'd rather be here alone,' I muttered.

'You know I wouldn't be happy leaving you here by yourself.' She paused. 'Anna, the other night you told me that you hated Sarah. That's an immature remark, darling, and not worthy of you. How could you possibly hate her? Time and again I've seen her try to be friends and I've never once seen you make the slightest move to meet her half way.' She touched my arm. 'Won't you try – even if it's only for my sake?' I made no reply. 'Will you, Anna?'

I took my eye off the road to glance at her. 'If I told you my side of the story, you wouldn't believe me.'

'Tell me, darling! Tell me why you're behaving the way you do. What's the reason?'

'Sarah's the one who started this, not me. It came entirely from her side. She—'

'Anna,' she interrupted, 'I've never heard Sarah be rude or unkind to you. On the contrary, she's gone out of her way to be friendly – and you've rebuffed her repeatedly. You've even struck her and she's borne you no ill will!'

'I refuse to discuss the matter any further!' I cried angrily, bitterness welling up. 'I've nothing more to say.' We drove in silence for the rest of the way.

When we returned to Wonderkloof, I ran upstairs to

fetch Chiang. I opened the door and found the room empty. The pink bedspread was rumpled and I could see the indentation where he'd slept. The rose-patterned curtains hung without movement. Sudden unreasoning fear gripped me and I scrambled over the wide window-sill and looked on to the pavings below. There was no sign of him. Panic stricken, I searched the house, franti-cally calling him.

Bella, Sannie and Hettie looked up as I opened the kitchen door. 'Have any of you seen Chiang?'

'No, Miss Anna.'

'Did one of you open the door and let him out?'

'No, Miss Anna.'

I ran into the sitting-room. Trina and Sarah were sit-ting on the sofa studying a rose catalogue. God knows what I must have looked like.

Trina looked up and leapt to her feet. 'What's wrong, Anna! What has happened?'

'Chiang's disappeared!'

'He must be somewhere, darling.' She looked re-lieved. 'He must be in the house.'

'He's nowhere in the house. He's gone, I tell you! He's gone! Someone took him out of my room!' I looked at Sarah. 'What have you done to him, Sarah? Where is he?'

She looked up, her face pale. 'How should I know where he is?' she said breathlessly.

'Where is he?' I cried, my voice too shrill. 'I can see by your face you know where he is!'

'Anna! Stop this nonsense at once! Why should Sarah know where he is?'

'She knows! I can see she knows. She's done some-thing to him!' I seized Sarah by the arms and shook her. 'Where is he?' I screamed. 'What have you done to him? Where is he! Where is he!'

'Anna!' Trina cried angrily. 'Stop being hysterical and pull yourself together at once!'

I looked around as Johan entered the room. He came over to me and took my arm. 'Come,' he said quietly, 'we'll go and search for him.'

I looked up, the tears streaming down my cheeks. 'How did you know he's missing?'

His face expressionless and without answering he led me from the room.

We searched for Chiang everywhere, systematically going through every room in the house – combing the garden and farm-yard.

At first I called for him repeatedly, but later lapsed into hopeless silence. Johan too was silent.

When we returned to the house it was dark. We entered through the court-yard and I stopped at the foot of the staircase.

'Thank you, Johan,' I looked at him dry eyed. 'I'll never see Chiang again – I know something's happened to him. Please tell Trina I don't want dinner.'

He suddenly caught me and held me tightly. 'For God's sake don't look like that,' he said huskily. My head was against his chest and I could hear the rhythmic beat of his heart; I could smell him and feel the warmth of his body. I wanted to cling to him. I wanted to pour my grief out in his arms. I wanted him to kiss me.

I tore myself away and ran upstairs.

Late that night the old house was silent and shrouded in darkness and I lay on my bed, staring in front of me, unable to sleep.

Suddenly there was a faint scratch on my door and I leapt off the bed, my heart pounding. 'Chiang!' I cried. 'Darling, you've come back to me! You've come back!' I ran and wrenched the door open.

Wolf stood in the doorway and he came in and licked

170

my hand. I went on my knees, put my arms around his neck and buried my face in his ruff, weeping as though my heart would break.

I never saw Chiang again. As suddenly as he entered my life – like a bright shaft of light – so swiftly he left it, leaving darkness and overwhelming loneliness.

Early the next morning at the first pale light of dawn, I traversed the paths and shadowed woods where I had so often walked with him, hoping by some miracle to find him. In the afternoon I searched again, Trina silently accompanying me. Later Wolf joined us, licking my hand before loping ahead.

'It's touching how fond he is of you.'

'It's because we both loved Chiang,' I said, my lips trembling.

'I'll give you another dog, darling.'

'No!' I cried. 'No, I don't want another dog. I never want to love anything again!' All I had loved I'd lost.

She gripped my arm. 'Come with us to Johannesburg, darling. It will do you good to get away. Why don't you stay there and spend a week or two with Maria.'

'No, Trina. I may still find him. I couldn't possibly go away now.'

On Wednesday I was again up at dawn. The air was soft and warm, and the sky above the peaks a deep glowing red, streaked with clouds like tongues of flame.

I walked slowly along the path next to Trina's walled garden. I passed the oak forest and stood on the ridge where Johan and I had paused a year ago. The slaves' grave-yard and pear and peach orchards were shrouded in grey mist. Only the tip of the tall clump of bamboo and the tops of the weeping-willows were visible.

I looked down as I felt Wolf lick my hand, and a moment later Johan came along the path towards me.

'Look at the sky, Johan. Isn't it beautiful?'

He looked up at the peaks and the flaming sky. 'Red sky in the morning – shepherd's warning!' he said sombrely.

'What time are you and Trina leaving?'

'We leave immediately after breakfast.' He looked at me, his narrow hand resting on Wolf's head. 'Anna.' His face appeared carved from stone in the strange reddish light.

'Yes?'

'Why don't you go?'

'Go?' I whispered with stiff lips.

'Yes, go. Why don't you leave Wonderkloof?'

I was so deeply wounded, I could feel the blood draining from my face. 'D'you want me to leave Wonderkloof?'

His hand clenched in Wolf's ruff and I heard the dog whine softly. 'Yes.' His voice sounded unnaturally loud. 'I want you to leave. I want you to go as soon as possible.'

'All right,' I said brokenly. 'I'll go.' I turned and ran back to the house, my eyes blinded with tears.

Chapter Twenty-three

I RAN TO my room, closed the door and leant against it, fighting to control my tears. Then I walked to the window and looked down on Trina's garden, drying my eyes.

Why, oh why, hadn't I spared myself this final bitter humiliation? Why hadn't I packed my bags weeks ago and left? Why had I so foolishly imagined that neither Johan nor Trina would ever tell me to leave Wonderkloof?

I sat at my desk. 'Dear Uncle Charles,' I wrote. 'May I come and live with you and Aunt Elizabeth?'

When Trina came to my room, I handed the letter to her. 'Will you post this for me?'

'Of course, darling.' I felt her studying me, and knew she'd noticed my tear-stained eyes. 'Why didn't you come down to breakfast this morning?'

'I wasn't hungry.'

'Darling, you're wearing yourself out looking for Chiang. Don't you think—'

'He's dead.' I interrupted. 'I won't look for him any more – I know I'll never see him again.'

She hesitated, then glanced at her watch. 'Goodness, I must go! Johannes will be waiting for me.' She kissed me and put her arm around my waist, drawing me to her.

'Try and patch things up with Sarah while we're away. Try and be friends with her, darling, for your own sake.'

I disengaged myself and kissed her lightly. 'Goodbye, Trina. Give my love to Maria and tell her she owes me a letter.'

Her face was bleak. 'I'll tell her.'

An hour later I went to the kitchen and found Bella and Hettie spring-cleaning the pantry.

'Now *Merrem*'s gorn for three days I do some cleaning up, Miss Anna,' Bella said importantly.

The pantry at Wonderkloof was like a large store-room. Pockets of sugar, beans, rice and flour stood under the stacked shelves. Rows of home-made canned fruit, jams and preserves glittered in labelled glass jars on the three top shelves. Mounds of unwrapped soap were drying out on the bottom shelf. Sannie came in carrying an armful of washed cannisters.

'Bella,' I said. 'I'll be busy for the next two days. Would you send my lunch and dinner to my room?'

'Yes, Miss Anna.'

Wolf met me in the hall and followed me, lying at my feet while I worked. By five o'clock I was jaded and tired and we went for a long walk. When we returned, I sat at my desk, typing until the early hours of the morning.

I was in a fever to set my house in order and leave Wonderkloof for ever. I knew I would never return.

I awoke next morning when Sannie brought in the tea tray. I put on my gown and poured out a cup of tea, sipping it as I sat on the wide window-sill. A slight north-westerly wind was blowing and once again an angry red sky glowed above the peaks. The air was unnaturally warm. The weather's changing, I thought. It's going to rain.

There was a light tap on my door.

'Come in,' I called.

The door opened and Sarah came in. She wore blue slacks and a long-sleeved white shirt.

'Get out!' I said quietly.

'Anna, please let me speak to you!'

'Get out! I don't want to hear what you've to say.'

Her lips trembled and she took a faltering step then hesitated uncertainly. 'Please listen to me – I've come to apologize.'

'Apologize!' I cried angrily. 'D'you think an apology could wipe out what you've done?'

'I know it's expecting too—'

'What did you do to Chiang?' I interrupted.

She burst into tears. 'I swear I did nothing to him. I swear it! I know I was sometimes cruel and unkind and can't blame you for thinking I might have done something – but I never went near him! I didn't even see him on Monday – I know as little about his disappearance as you do.'

'I don't believe you!'

'Please believe me. Please!'

She caught my hand and I snatched it away. 'Don't touch me!'

She wrung her hands. 'Oh, what must I do? How can I make you believe me?' She stared at me, her deep blue eyes blazing into mine. 'Look at me, Anna. Look into my eyes! I solemnly swear that I did nothing to him.'

'Why have you been treating me like this, Sarah? Why have you made my life a misery?'

'I was jealous of you,' she said in a low voice.

'Jealous of me!' I cried with scornful disbelief. 'Come, you can hardly expect me to believe that.'

'It's true,' her voice was still low. 'I was insanely jealous of you.'

'Sarah, you're without exception the most beautiful

woman I've seen: you're also wealthy – and happily married. In comparison – I've no money, nobody would look at me twice and I've neither a husband nor a lover. Do you seriously expect me to believe that you're jealous of me?'

'Everybody likes you more than me,' she muttered almost inaudibly.

'You're talking nonsense!'

'It's not nonsense, it's true! Johan talks and laughs with you as he never does with me. Trina puts her arm around you and calls you darling. *Tant'* Bettie kisses you.' It was like the bursting of a dam. 'The servants like you more – I can feel it! Look how Lettie asked you to be Violet's godmother, and Bella baked you a cake. Even he!' She pointed at Wolf, curled next to my desk. 'Even he loves you and ignores me.'

'That's because he loved Chiang.'

'Pieter hardly ever speaks to me, but I often hear him talking to you in your room. He's always pestering you to go for walks but has never once asked me.'

'Sarah, all my life I've spent the Christmas holidays at Wonderkloof. In a way I'm like a member of the family. Johan always called my mother Aunt Lorrie – he and Pieter look upon me as a cousin. Trina's my godmother and has known me all my life – she's always called me darling.'

She was still crying softly. 'I'm only trying to explain how out of things I feel.'

'Trina loves you, Sarah. She's always telling me how proud she is of you.'

'Anna.' She looked at me pleadingly, her eyes wet with tears. 'Will you forgive me? I know it's a lot to expect. I didn't go to Johannesburg because I wanted to find an opportunity of apologizing. I've been so ashamed – can you forgive me?' Her lips quivered.

'Please, Anna!' I looked at her silently. 'I'm sorry,' she whispered. 'I suppose it's too much to expect.' She turned away.

'All right,' I said grudgingly. 'I'm prepared to accept your apology, on condition you tell Trina and Johan what you've done.'

Her face was radiant. 'I'll do it! I promise! I'll tell them tomorrow night and you'll hear every word.' She grasped my hand and this time I allowed her to hold it. 'Thank you, Anna. I'll never forget how generous you've been.' She smiled at me uncertainly. 'Can't we get out of the house and spend the day together?'

I glanced doubtfully at my typewriter. 'I don't think I can spare the time: I've so much work to do.'

'Forget it for today!' she cried impulsively. 'We've never got to know each other – I know it's been my fault. Please spend the day with me!'

My room suddenly closed in on me like a prison.

I shrugged and smiled. 'All right, let's get up to the Kloof for the day.'

She clapped her hands, her eyes bright with excitement. 'I'll run down and tell Bella to make a picnic lunch.'

'Tell her to put in two bottles of beer, and pack our food in separate knapsacks.'

'I'll go and tell her at once.' She kissed me shyly. 'Thank you, Anna.'

When we entered the kitchen after breakfast, the two knapsacks were lying on the table.

Bella beamed at us. 'Good-morning, Miss Anna. The food is packed, and I put in two bottles of beer, like you say. There ham and chicken. I sorry I don't know yesterday you was going for a picnic, then I make something extra nice.' She looked at me and folded her hands, her eyes watering. '*Merrem* heppy if she see you and Miss Sarah now.'

'Yes, I think she would be.'

Wolf wagged his tail and followed us into the court-yard. Sarah stopped and looked at him with a slight frown. 'Don't let him come with us! I know he hates me.'

I stroked his head. 'He'll be so disappointed.'

'Please, Anna! Let him come some other time. I don't want anything to spoil today.'

'I'm sorry, Wolf.' I tweaked his ears. 'Stay!' I said firmly. He looked at me with his dark eyes intently fixed on my face and barked.

I could still hear him barking when we reached the shed on the farm-yard where the jeep was parked. We clambered in and Sarah tossed her handbag on to the back seat.

'Why on earth are you taking your bag?' I asked.

She lifted an amused eyebrow. 'I can see that you think I'm vain. I admit I wouldn't think of going out for the day without my bag.'

She reversed the jeep and drove across the uneven farmyard, avoiding the hens and geese. She stopped at the gate and I jumped down and opened it for her.

She handled the jeep competently over the rough rutted road. In places the heavy winter rains had poured down the banks, scouring out deep ditches through which we crawled at a snail's pace. When we reached the old Cape laurel, she parked between two granite boulders in the shade and we scrambled out, shouldering our knapsacks.

The day was hot and sultry with a slight strengthening of the north-westerly wind. Sarah walked ahead of me on the narrow stony footpath, her slim body moving with supple ease. Even her body's perfect, I thought, with a touch of bitterness. We'd walked about half a mile when I called to her to stop.

'What's wrong?' she asked, looking at me in surprise, her cheeks flushed.

'I thought I caught a glimpse of something pink beyond those sugarbushes on the left.' I caught her hand. 'Come with me, it may be a patch of Trina's pink *pypies*.'

They covered a quarter of an acre of *veld*, growing in their thousands. We stared speechlessly at the carpet of long-stemmed delicate blooms moving restlessly in the strengthening wind.

'Oh, Sarah! We must pick a bunch of these for Trina on our way back, and if it's fine on Sunday, we must bring her here – she won't believe us unless she sees this with her own eyes.'

'It's beautiful!' Her eyes were shining and her mouth slightly open in wonder.

'Trina will be pleased that we're friends,' I said impulsively.

When we reached the path she stopped and looked at me. 'Why was Trina so fond of your mother?'

'There were quite a few reasons.' I laughed. 'My mother and father were one of Trina's successful efforts at matchmaking (and you know what an inveterate matchmaker she is!). That alone gave her a proprietary interest in them. She and my mother also had a lot in common. They liked the same books, the same people and had the same sense of humour. My mother was restful, she was quite unlike Trina: I think that's why they got on so well together. I remember Johan once saying to her, "Aunt Lorrie, you're the most restful woman I've ever met".'

'Oh.'

I grinned and patted her back. 'Good heavens! Don't look so serious about it!'

She smiled faintly. 'You must be very like your mother.'

'No, not really. I think I'm fairly restful, but I'm quick-tempered. I never once heard my mother raise her voice in all the years we lived together.'

We were again climbing the steep slope and I reached out and took her handbag. 'Let me carry your bag for a while.'

She snatched it back. 'No!' she cried sharply, then quickly smiled. 'I'm sorry, I didn't mean to be rude. If I'm stupid enough to take my bag the least I should do is carry it myself.'

'It's certainly heavy enough! What's in it?'

She wrinkled her nose and laughed. 'My make-up! By the time we reach the Kloof I'll be a mess. When we get there I'll want to clean my face.'

It was midday when we reached the grove of trees above the waterfall. We sat in the shade on the bank of the stream and scooped our hands in the icy water. Sarah leant against a rock and took out her mirror, critically inspecting her face and I walked to the edge of the cliff and watched the clear water cascading down the rock face. I cautiously peered over the edge and saw that the *waboom* was dead. Drops of water glittered like diamonds on the stiff dried brown leaves.

'The *waboom*'s dead,' I called. 'You must tell Johan.'

She ran a comb through her hair, put the mirror and comb in her handbag and snapped it shut, then placed it on a rock at her feet. She jumped up and came over to me.

'Let me see.'

She knelt next to me, looked over the edge and I saw her glance quickly to the left and stiffen.

'What's wrong, Sarah?'

'There's someone there!'

'Nonsense!'

'There is, I tell you,' she whispered urgently. 'And there's something lying on the stones – it looks like an old shirt drying in the sun.' She scrambled to her feet, her eyes dilated and her face deathly pale. 'D'you think it could be Adonis?' she asked breathlessly.

I was infected by her agitation and my pulse quickened. 'If it is, we must get our things and go back at once!'

'I'm sure it's a shirt. You have a look.'

I knelt and leaned carefully over the edge. 'I can't see a thing.'

'Not there!' she whispered impatiently. 'It's more to the left.'

I leaned further forward, craning my head to the left – and then she pushed me.

As I plunged headlong over the cliff my secret was torn from me. 'Johan!' I screamed. My agonized shriek echoed through the lonely Kloof like the cry of a lost soul.

Chapter Twenty-four

THE *waboom* saved my life.

I crashed sickeningly into the centre of it, gasping as the breath was knocked from my body. I clutched at the brittle branches, the hard dry leaves crackling under my hands as I frantically sought purchase to try and save myself. Then it tore away from the cliff and I fell a further twenty feet on to the rounded stones below. My left leg doubled under me and I heard it snap like a dry twig. I screamed and fainted.

Regaining consciousness was like rising from the dark depths of a pool. First there was darkness, then swirling twilight, and finally glaring daylight and the blazing realization of what had happened. I found myself lying on my back at the foot of the cliff. A branch of the *waboom* obscured my vision and I put up my hands pushing it aside. I looked up and forty feet above saw Sarah's white face peering at me over the ledge.

'You pushed me!' I cried.

She put her shoulder to the rock next to her and I saw her body straining against it as she applied every ounce of strength to dislodge it.

With a stab of terror, I realized that she intended murdering me. Sobbing with fright, I scrambled backwards like a crab dragging my leg, and heard the bones grind. Sweating, nauseous and half-fainting, I was unable to drag myself more than a few feet. A second later the rock crashed deafeningly next to me and I cried out in panic.

Panting with terror, I looked up and saw no sign of her, but a moment later she was silhouetted against the skyline, her shirt brilliantly white in the noon sun and her long black hair streaming in the wind.

I shall remember that moment all my life. That, and the bright flash as the sun's rays reflected off the revolver she was pointing at me. Now I knew what she had kept in her bag.

She fired a shot. The sound was deafening, echoing and re-echoing through the Kloof. She fired again, then turned and vanished, and I knew she was climbing down the precipitous path. I turned and lay on my right side so that I could keep my eyes fixed on the deeply shaded glade where I knew she must appear. Trembling and numb with shock I awaited my executioner.

Time stood still, and I thought she'd never come, yet when she did, it was sudden and unexpected and a shock jolted my body in a spasm of fear. She paused at the edge of the pool and I saw the reflection of her white shirt in the water. Then she picked her way as fastidiously as a cat across the rounded stones. I watched her approach, apathetically accepting my fate. There was no fierce rebellion against the termination of my life – I awaited her with hopeless resignation.

A movement made me look beyond her. A figure emerged from the glade and ran barefooted, swiftly and silently across the smooth stones. She was a few yards from me, her eyes glazed and her face dead white; as she lifted the revolver, he flung his arms around her waist and pinned her arms to her side. They struggled in deathly silence and I heard his laboured breathing as he strove to hold her. Suddenly she flung her head back and screamed – a frustrated shriek of rage.

'Give me the gun, my *Nooi*,' Adonis panted. 'You not shoot the *Klein Nooi*. *Baas* Johan not like it.'

'Let me go, you filthy beast! Let me go or I'll kill you! I'll shoot both of you! D'you hear me? Let me go!'

'The gun, my *Nooi*. Give Adonis the gun.'

She screamed again and started fighting with the ferocity of a wild animal. He grunted and breathed heavily as he strained to control her. Suddenly she flung herself sideways; he lost his footing and they slowly toppled forwards; as he fell on top of her I heard the muffled sound of a shot. They lay so still, I thought they were dead.

Then he got to his knees and slowly rose to his feet, staggering as he did so. He looked down at her; his chest heaving and his mouth slack. She was lying on her face. Her silky black hair fanned over the rocks, exposing the tender white nape of her neck.

'She dead, *Klein Nooi*. She dead!' he cried hoarsely, his breath rasping in his throat. 'She dead! I kill *Baas* Johan's wife!'

'She may not be dead, Adonis. Turn her over and see if she's still breathing.'

'No, *Klein Nooi*!' he cried shrilly, backing away. 'No! I not touch her!'

I tried to drag myself forward but the effort made me fall back, half-fainting. 'Pick me up, Adonis, and put me next to her. I'll see if she's alive.'

He put his arms under my body and lifted me gently – the stench of his sweat was in my nostrils. He placed me next to her and I lifted her head and looked into her white face and sightless eyes; then I let her face sink back on to the stones and spread her hair as it was before.

'She's dead, Adonis.'

He wrung his hands and gave a gutteral cry. The blazing midday sun beat down mercilessly and I could feel it sapping my strength. 'Carry me to the shade, Adonis. Put me on the grass under the trees,' I gasped.

This time when he lifted me, I fainted.

When I regained consciousness, he was squatting on the grass bank next to me, looking at me anxiously. His bearded face was grey and gaunt. Sweat beaded his forehead and trickled down his hollow cheeks. His filthy ragged clothes hung on his emaciated body – he was dirty and half-starved.

'I see *Baas* Johan's *Nooi* push you, *Klein Nooi*. I hide in the bushes. When she go to shoot you, I follow.'

'Thank you, Adonis, you saved my life.'

He didn't hear me. He buried his face in his hands. 'Oh, I's bad! I bad! First I kill Annekie and now I kill *Baas* Johan's wife.'

'It was an accident.' Nauseous and shaking, I leaned over and retched painfully.

'I love Annekie, *Klein Nooi*. When I merry her and she come to Wonderkloof, she the prettiest coloured girl on the farm and all the *volk* jealous of me, *Klein Nooi*: and I proud because I know they want her, and I know I the only man what Annekie ever have – she let no one touch her.'

'If you loved her, why were you cruel to her?' Talking made me faint and I started retching again.

'She my shame, *Klein Nooi*.' His voice was so low I could hardly hear him. 'She always my shame. One night there big party and we drink and dance – and I see all the *volk* look at Annekie and I proud.' He looked away and stared across the dark pool. 'I drink too much wine and when I wake up, Annekie lie next to me. Her nose is broken, her teeth's knocked out and she got a

185

black eye. I take her in my arms, *Klein Nooi*, and I say, "Who done it, Annekie? Tell me who done it and I kill him!"' His eyes were now fixed on mine. 'And she look at me, *Klein Nooi*, and she say "You done it, Adonis."' He broke into hoarse strangling sobs. 'I done it! I, Adonis, done it!'

I was unable to speak. I clenched my teeth to stop them chattering, but couldn't control the violent trembling of my body. Waves of nausea overwhelmed me. The numbness was leaving my leg and hot throbbing pain breaking through.

'Annekie then my shame, *Klein Nooi*. Everyone what see her face know that I, Adonis, done it.'

I retched again and fell back half-fainting, no longer listening to him. I lay with my eyes closed, groaning softly, the tears trickling down my cheeks.

'*Klein Nooi*.'

I opened my eyes. 'Yes, Adonis?'

'You going to die, *Klein Nooi*.' It was a statement, not a question.

'Yes, Adonis. I'll die unless you fetch help.'

He wrung his hands. 'They hang me if they catch me, *Klein Nooi*! If I fetch help they tell police.'

I closed my eyes. I must have lost consciousness because when I opened them again he was staring at me, his face haggard and his burning eyes fixed on my face.

'Don't die, *Klein Nooi*!' It was a cry. 'I fetch *Baas* Johan. He not tell police. I go fetch *Baas* Johan.'

'He's not there. He's in Johannesburg.'

He cried out as though I'd struck him.

He watched me for a few minutes, then stripped off his jacket. 'You cold, *Klein Nooi*.' He put it over me. 'My coat dirty and not smell good. But you cold, you shivering – you die of cold.'

'Thank you,' I whispered.

186

I was no longer able to clench my jaws and stop my teeth from chattering like castanets. Submerged in waves of pain I lay with my eyes closed, moaning softly and sometimes crying out when the pain became unbearable. When I opened my eyes again I was alone.

The keening wind was stronger and the shadows in the Kloof slowly lengthened. A rock rabbit moved on a rock nearby and stood on its hindlegs, its nose wriggling inquisitively and its small shiny eyes riveted on my face. A blue kingfisher flashed across the pool. A hawk, hovering in the sky, plummeted like a stone. When I turned my head I could see Sarah sprawled on the stones, her black silky hair blown by the wind.

The loneliness and deep silence of the Kloof was like a tomb.

I slipped into nightmares. There was always pain – and cold; icy coldness which gripped me with clammy fingers.

I heard Adonis, say, 'She my shame, *Klein Nooi* – she always my shame.'

'You must be very like your mother, Anna.'

'Yes, I want you to leave Wonderkloof. I want you to go as soon as possible,' – and his face was like carved stone in the red light.

'Look at me, Anna. Look into my eyes!'

I awoke to hear the ominous roar of the wind and could see the frenzied movements of the trees above the waterfall. Looking up at the black swollen clouds, I cried silently, knowing that I would surely die.

Chapter Twenty-five

THE NIGHTMARE CHANGED and I was no longer in the lonely Kloof, but in a small white aseptic room struggling frantically to breathe – each rasping breath torturing my pain-racked body.

Trina was there, holding my hand.

'I'm going to die,' I cried hoarsely.

Her face swam into focus, fiercely determined. 'Don't give in, Anna. You're not going to die. You're going to live!'

And my brain echoed, you're going to live, you're going to live, you're going to live.

There were times when Trina wasn't there – then I was afraid and cried out, for her. 'She'll be back soon.'

She'll be back. She'll be back. She'll be back.

Sometimes a man's pale bespectacled face floated into my vision. 'You say Adonis fell on top of her and the gun went off?'

'Yes,' I gasped.

'Must you ask her these questions now?'

'Yes, I'm afraid we must, Mrs de Villiers.'

'Have you any idea why she wanted to kill you?'

'No!'

I felt Trina's grip tighten on my hand and her angry

voice cried out, 'Stop torturing the child. I insist that you leave us now.'

Again I was hurtling over the cliff. 'Johan!' I screamed. And I heard his name echo and re-echo through the lonely Kloof.

Johan! Johan! Johan!

I opened my eyes one day and the nightmare was over. I lay in a small room breathing easily, the white gauze curtains billowed gently in the breeze and Trina was sitting beside my bed holding my hand.

'Where am I?' I asked, surprised at the faintness of my voice.

'You're in hospital, darling.'

'Then I'm not going to die?'

She gripped my hand and lifted her chin, her eyes bright. 'No, darling. You're not going to die.'

'Who found me?' I whispered.

'Hush, Anna. Don't talk anymore. Go to sleep, darling. Sleep as much as you can and get well.'

A week later I asked her the same question. 'Who found me?'

'Johannes found you.'

She avoided my eyes and I knew she shared my secret. How many times she must have heard me calling for him. How many times I must have told her that I loved him.

'But when did he find me, Trina? He was with you in Johannesburg.'

'He found you that same night. It was one of those strange things. Johannes suddenly returned to Cape Town. At the time, when I got his message, I was very annoyed. You know how uncommunicative he can be. When I asked what had made him change his plans, he told me he knew something was wrong.'

I looked at her squarely. 'I screamed for him when I fell over the cliff – perhaps he heard me.'

189

She caught my hand and kissed it. 'Perhaps he did, darling. Perhaps it was telepathy.' She released my hand and blew her nose. 'When Johannes reached Wonderkloof, Bella heard the car and met him on the *stoep*, she told him that you'd gone to the Kloof and he took a lantern and left at once. He found the jeep parked under the laurel and half-way up to the Kloof met Adonis in such a hysterical state that he was incapable of speaking. They carried you to the car and reached it just before the storm broke. Johannes then drove you straight to hospital.'

'What's happened to Adonis?'

'He's in prison awaiting trial.'

'I hope he won't be hanged.' I looked at her. 'How's Johan, Trina?' She shook her head and remained silent.

I got several letters from Uncle Charles. When I told Trina that I intended living with him, she merely nodded.

The thought of leaving hospital and returning to Wonderkloof filled me with dread, and she sensed this. 'You know how Johannes always says I'm a great organizer,' she smiled. 'Well, I've been doing a little organizing on your behalf, darling.'

'Oh,' I looked at her with raised eyebrows. 'What have you arranged for me?'

'As you know Maria is coming down for Gert and Bettie's thirtieth wedding anniversary. She'll be staying at Mooi Vlei for three weeks. Bettie has suggested that you should stay with them when you leave hospital and I think it's a good idea. How d'you feel about it?'

'Yes, I'd like that,' I tried not to look too pleased.

'I've booked your flight to London so that you can fly to Johannesburg with Maria when she leaves – that means she'll be able to look after you on the plane. I'm not happy about your travelling on crutches. I only hope you'll manage by yourself on the flight to London.'

'I'll be all right.'

190

'I would like to have gone with you but I can't leave Johannes – he needs me.'

'Is he any better?'

'He sits in his study, night after night. If only he'd talk about it, Anna.' She shook her head. 'At the moment no one can help him.'

She sat more erect, and looked at me, her eyes soft. 'Don't stay away too long. Come back to us one day, darling.' I averted my face.

She cleared her throat. 'There's something else, Anna.'

The tone of her voice made me look at her quickly. 'What?' I asked apprehensively.

'There'll be an inquest. You'll have to give evidence.' My heart started to race. 'Don't let it upset you too much, darling,' she said compassionately. 'Try not to worry about it.'

I clutched the bedclothes. 'When – when will they hold the inquest?' I stammered.

'The week after next. You'll be at Mooi Vlei.'

Trina, soberly dressed in a brown suit, fetched me on the day of the inquest. The court was crowded and I sat with my head bowed, conscious that people were staring at us. Trina sat next to me, holding my hand until I was called to give evidence. I was allowed to sit in the witness box. It wasn't comfortable on the hard high-backed chair with my leg in plaster stretched out in front of me. I sat very straight with my hands tightly clenched in my lap.

The advocate was a pale bespectacled young man whose appearance was vaguely familiar. 'You say you were both above the cliff – you were kneeling, looking over the edge, and she pushed you?'

'Yes.'

191

'You didn't slip and fall?'

'No, she pushed me.'

'What happened when you found yourself lying at the bottom of the cliff?'

'I shouted and accused her of pushing me. Then I saw her trying to dislodge a rock on the edge of the cliff, so that it would fall on me and crush me.' I swallowed painfully.

'And then?'

'I managed to move back a few feet before it fell.'

I was forced to relive everything I'd endured. Question after question was remorselessly fired at me. Often the tears ran down my cheeks and I quickly wiped them away, biting my lips to control myself.

The magistrate sometimes quietly intervened. 'You say Adonis struggled with her, lost his balance, and fell on top of her?'

'Yes.'

'He at no time succeeded in wresting the revolver from her?'

'No.'

'You say Adonis saved your life. If he hadn't arrived when he did, pinning her arms to her side, she'd have shot you?'

'Yes,' I said in a low voice, hardly able to speak. 'She would have shot me.'

'Have you any idea why she'd want to shoot you?'

'No.'

When I rejoined Trina I sat looking down, crying silently, oblivious to what was taking place in court. Once I glanced at Johan, sitting three seats away, his face hard and as expressionless as a mask.

In a dream I heard the verdict 'Accidental Death'. Keeping my head down, I limped on my crutches out of the crowded court. During the drive to Mooi Vlei I sat

192

huddled against the door, unable to speak. That night I awoke screaming.

The three weeks at Mooi Vlei passed quickly, and daily I became more adept on my crutches.

I was listless, easily tired and had moments of depression and despair when I leaned heavily on Maria and Trina to buoy my spirits. Trina came to see me every day.

'I can't make the child eat,' *Tant'* Bettie said. 'Look at her, she's nothing but skin and bone! She doesn't eat enough to sustain a bird.'

Trina flashed me a quick smile. 'Don't worry about Anna. She'll eat in time.'

The day before I left, she came to my room and helped me pack. 'All your other things are packed, darling, and I've sent them off by sea. They should arrive soon after you reach The Oaks.' She fidgeted with the things on my dressing-table and then came and sat next to me on the bed. 'Anna.'

'Yes?'

'I'll never cease to reproach myself for not believing you when you tried to tell me about Sarah. I didn't even listen to you.'

'I can't blame you.'

'I've known you all my life, darling – how could I have doubted you!' She rose and walked to the window. 'I'll always remember the night I told you what a good friend Bettie is – how you came and stood next to me in front of the mirror and said, "I've one just as good".'

'I have, Trina! I have! If you hadn't sat with me day after day holding my hand, willing me to live and forcing me to fight, I'd not be alive now. There was no will left in me.' I added.

'I failed you, Anna! I failed you when you needed me most, and it will haunt me all my life.' She came back and gripped my shoulders, looking down at me. 'Come back to us one day, darling.'

I looked down and the tears splashed on to my clenched hands.

'I'll never come back,' I sobbed. 'Never.'

Chapter Twenty-six

UNCLE CHARLES and Aunt Elizabeth met me at London Airport. My appearance was obviously a shock and they exchanged a quick alarmed glance. It was snowing lightly and the icy biting wind penetrated my clothes, entering my very soul. The cold white landscape filled me with despondency and despair and I was silent during the drive to Surrey.

When we reached The Oaks, Aunt Elizabeth took me to my bedroom and lit the fire. 'Why don't you go to bed, Anna? You're looking tired.'

I smiled wanly. 'I think I shall.'

Aunt Elizabeth had no difficulty in persuading me to go to bed but she couldn't induce me to leave it. Like Johan's grandmother, I'd found a haven and refuge from the world. Here there was warmth and security. I no longer needed to fend for myself. There were no decisions to make or problems to face.

I came to know every tile on the fireplace and each flower on the Chinese carpet. When I closed my eyes I could visualize the misty sentimental picture above the fireplace, of a thatch-roofed cottage covered with roses, standing near a stream.

My crutches were propped against the chair next to my bed; sometimes I stood at the window looking on to the kitchen garden and heard Hammet the gardener whistling softly while he pottered in the greenhouse. At times it was snowing – bleak and cold and I shivered and hobbled back to the warmth and security of my bed.

Aunt Elizabeth came into my room every morning and smiled cheerfully. 'How about getting up today?'

'Not today. I'm not feeling well. Perhaps tomorrow.'

'Why don't you get up for a short while and come downstairs? I'll light the fire in the study.'

'No, thanks. I'd like to stay in bed today.'

Every day she cleaned out the fireplace, relayed the fire and lit it. She carried up my breakfast and lunch, and Uncle Charles brought my dinner in the evening. I spared no thought for them and lay hour after hour disinterestedly watching television.

Uncle Charles came into my room early one morning when I'd been in bed for two and a half weeks. He kissed me and then sat in the chair next to my bed and looked at me rather sternly.

'Are you getting up today?'

'No, Uncle Charles. Maybe tomorrow.'

'I think you should today, my dear,' he said quietly.

'I'm not feeling well.'

'Anna.'

I looked at him quickly. 'Yes, Uncle Charles?'

'Elizabeth and I know you've been through a bad time. We love you and will do all we can to help you.' He paused. 'But neither of us is prepared to lift a finger to help you run away from life.' He stood up. 'We'll expect you down for breakfast in half an hour. Elizabeth is busy in the kitchen and will be glad of your help.'

I flushed painfully. 'I'll get up at once.'

He smiled and nodded.

'I'm sorry,' I whispered.

'We all have problems to face in our lives, Anna.

196

Never run away from them.' He patted my arm and kissed me.

I discarded my crutches a week before Christmas and trailed around the house listlessly watching Aunt Elizabeth decorating the Christmas tree, and hanging up the holly. I wore the same clothes day after day and used no make-up, my lank hair uncombed and lustreless. I spent hours crouched in a chair looking at television.

My thoughts often returned to Wonderkloof. I could see the Persian rugs scattered about the yellow-wood floors; the wine brocaded curtains in the sitting-room reflected in the polished surface of Trina's Queen Anne desk; and the lustrous green-gold curtains in the dining-room that exactly matched the low-cut gown of Johan's great-grandmother, Gertrude Barton – I thought of her level grey eyes, so like Johan's.

My greatest interest was the weekly letter from Trina which was always evocative and entertaining. A week before Christmas she wrote—

'Last night Johannes and I were having coffee when Julian came in and went over to Johannes who was standing by the fireplace, his face so strained and thin. Julian took his arm and led him out of the room. I've never loved Julian more than at that moment. There have been times when I didn't approve of him, but he's not Gert and Bettie's son for nothing. He, more than anyone, could help Johannes at this time.'

The snow melted in February and though it was cold and rained incessantly, there was a difference in the air. In March Uncle Charles took me into the garden and showed me the first crocuses. He smiled and put his arm around my shoulders. 'Spring's just around the corner.'

With its approach there was a stirring and uplifting of my spirits. Aunt Elizabeth taught me to cook. I went for short walks with Uncle Charles, sharing the adventure

197

of watching the garden awaken. As the weather improved we spent all our time digging, planting and weeding. Their patience and love slowly healed my wounds.

But it was Oliver who brought me alive. Oliver Bates, the architect who lived with his mother, Lady Bates, in the cottage next door. Sarcastic, rude, self-opinioned and blasphemous, he was a stimulant and an abrasive.

I saw little of him during the first five months at The Oaks. Occasionally he brought me a book and sat with me; but it was easy to see that he found the presence of Uncle Charles and Aunt Elizabeth irksome. When we were alone he was derisive and ironical.

'My God, don't you know anything about modern art and music? Don't you ever read!'

'Of course I do. I read a lot – and stop bullying me.'

Whenever he lent me a book he encouraged me to express my views, if only to ridicule my opinions. 'You're so god-damned sentimental, Anna. Everything has to be wrapped up in cellophane and tied with a pink ribbon. Why can't you be realistic?'

'You're cynical and hard, Oliver.'

His hair was crisp and fair and his chiselled face could have decorated a coin – his chin was as lean and obstinate as Johan's.

When the weather improved I often spent the evening in his study listening to music and reading, while he worked at his desk. At ten o'clock I made coffee and then he joined me on the sofa and we talked.

He was at home nearly every night during the week, but away practically every weekend.

'Where d'you go every weekend?'

'Mind your own business, Anna.'

One evening he looked up as I entered the study. The sight of me seemed to irritate him more than usual and his brows drew together. 'Must you always wear that awful skirt. Haven't you any other clothes?'

'What's wrong with it?' I stared at him defensively.

'Everything! It's too long, it hangs on you like a sack, and you've sat a seat in it.' He flung his pencil on the desk and his chair scraped as he pushed it back. He strode across and pushed me towards the mirror. 'For God's sake, look at yourself! Look at your hair! Why don't you do something about it? Why don't you wear some make-up?'

I looked at myself in the mirror and cringed. Lank, uncombed hair hung about my pale face. My grubby jersey was bagging at the elbows. I was grateful that I couldn't see my skirt.

'If there's one thing I can't stand it's a frowsy woman.'

'I'm going home!' I cried angrily. 'And I shan't come back!' I added as I ran out of the room and banged the door.

Aunt Elizabeth crinkled her eyes when I came down to help her with the breakfast the next morning. 'I like your suit. I haven't seen it before.'

'I shortened the skirt last night.'

Uncle Charles wandered aimlessly into the kitchen. 'Is breakfast nearly ready?' He glanced at me. 'You're looking very smart this morning, my dear.'

I carried the dish of bacon and kidneys through to the dining-room. 'Aunt Elizabeth,' I said as I sat down. 'I want to go to Oxted this morning and have my hair washed, cut and set.' I felt Uncle Charles dart another glance in my direction.

'I'll ring up and make an appointment for you.'

I hesitated and blushed. 'Is there a place where they can show me how to make up my eyes?'

'There is. I'll book an appointment for you as soon as

your hair's done.' As she passed, she stopped and hugged me impulsively.

That evening I gazed at myself for a long time before going to see Oliver, still unaccustomed to my new appearance. I was wearing a well-cut green and brown houndstooth suit which Trina had given me a year ago. The skirt was now fashionably short. My hairstyle was short and sophisticated and my skilfully made-up eyes looked twice their usual size.

I was self-conscious and nervous when I tapped on the door and walked into Oliver's study.

'I thought you weren't coming back,' he said without looking up.

He was sitting at the desk, his head bent over his work and the light above him burnishing his fair hair.

When I made no reply, he looked up. His eyebrows rose. 'Jesus, what have you done to yourself!' He pushed his chair back and came to me, looking me over. He took my face in his hands and turned it towards the light studying it without comment. He looked at my hair and appraised my suit. 'Not bad,' he said softly. 'Not bad at all! Turn around and let's see what you look like from the back.' I turned around self-consciously. 'Not bad,' he repeated. I smiled shyly. 'Sit down.' he said irritably, 'and stop looking so coy. I've bought two tickets for that controversial play at the Aldwych. Now that you're looking respectable, I'll take you.'

'You might at least ask me if I'd like to go.'

His rare brilliant smile lit his face. 'Don't come if you don't want to.'

Chapter Twenty-seven

IN APRIL Trina wrote: 'You asked me about Adonis. I didn't write to you when his trial took place as I felt it wiser not to mention it at the time. He was tried in January and sentenced to fifteen years' imprisonment. As I prophesied it was proved that he was drunk when he killed Annekie and not aware of what he was doing. It's only this fact which saved his neck. Julian went with Johannes to the trial. He told me that Adonis broke down. Poor Johannes was silent and depressed for weeks. However, he's looking better. It's eight months since that terrible day at the Kloof, and he's beginning to look less strained. Julian's been a good friend and sees him nearly every day. You too, darling, sound much happier.

'Lettie was married last Saturday in the last stages of pregnancy. Bella managed to do something about the wedding-dress, but the poor child looked like a ship in full sail. I still think that young carpenter is much too good for her. The reception was held in the big packing-shed: Johannes and I were both present. Bella, majestic in purple satin, presided over the proceedings like a queen. *Ou* Christiaan became so drunk that he was put in a wheelbarrow and taken home.

'James tells me he'll be in London for three weeks in

July and I've asked him to look you up so that I can have first-hand news of you. I miss you so much darling.'

But in July, Uncle Charles, Aunt Elizabeth and I spent a month in Italy.

I returned from this holiday tanned and well.

'You're looking quite different,' Aunt Elizabeth said on the evening of our return. We were sitting at the kitchen table having supper.

'I feel different.' I looked at them and smiled. 'I'm cured, thanks to you. I never thought I'd feel free and happy again. I'm so ashamed when I think how badly I behaved the first few months I was here.'

Uncle Charles smiled kindly. 'You didn't behave badly, my dear. You were unhappy and still suffering from shock.'

'Are you going to see Oliver this evening?' Aunt Elizabeth asked. She still cherished romantic dreams about Oliver and me.

'Yes, I'll go and see him when we've finished washing up.'

I tapped on his door at half past eight and found him sitting at his desk.

He greeted me more affably than usual. 'Well, how did you enjoy yourself?' He turned down the music and came to sit next to me on the sofa.

'I enjoyed every minute of it. I revelled in the hot sun. At Rapallo I swam every day – you can see how sunburnt I am.'

'Yes, you're looking well.' He absently fingered the material of my dress. 'Not a bad dress you're wearing.'

'Uncle Charles bought it for me in Rome. I loved Rome, Oliver! I'm so glad you lent me that book – I knew exactly what to see.'

'Did you enjoy Florence?'

'Very much. I agree with you about Michelangelo's David – I was unprepared for the impact it made on me.'

He was studying my face. 'Tell me what happened to you,' he said suddenly.

'Where – in Florence?'

'No, in South Africa.'

I stared at him feeling myself go pale. 'In South Africa?' I whispered.

'Yes. What happened to you before you came to live here? It must have been something pretty grim to make you look like you did.'

I clasped my hands and tears pricked my eyelids. 'Oh, Oliver, must I?'

'Yes, tell me,' he said with quiet insistence, putting his hand over mine.

I sat in silence. Then in a low faltering voice told him everything from beginning to end. When I was finished I drew a shuddering breath, looked down at his hand covering my clenched fists, and tried to control my tears.

'Quite a story,' he said softly. He lifted my chin compelling me to look into his eyes, his expression unreadable as he studied my face. My eyes filled with tears and I was unable to stop my lips trembling. He put his arm around my waist drawing me to him and kissed me, gently forcing my mouth open. He caressed my throat with cool fingers, as his hand slipped under my collar towards my breast, I instinctively stiffened.

'Relax, Anna, I'm not going to bite you.'

'It's not the biting I'm worried about!'

He laughed and looked at me, still holding me close. 'What are you afraid of?' I hung my head and said nothing. 'Don't you like being kissed?'

'I'm different,' I muttered.

'What d'you mean – in what way are you different?'

'I don't feel anything when I'm kissed. There's something missing in my make-up.'

'Are you trying to tell me that you're one of those frigid women?' When I made no reply, he laughed shortly. 'What a lot of goddamned poppycock! You're no more frigid than I am.' He took his arm away but remained sitting close to me. 'I'll tell you what's wrong with you, my girl,' he said, with a rather unpleasant smile. 'You were infatuated with that clodhopper.'

'What clodhopper?' I whispered.

'That beefy farming rugby player who got married while you and his mother were staying at The Oaks last year – the husband of this Sarah you've been telling me about.'

'D'you m-mean Johan de Villiers?' I stammered.

'You know whom I mean, my girl. My God, you should have seen your face the night my mother and I dined at The Oaks, when you'd just heard he was married. You sat there looking like a ghost.' He looked me up and down. 'You're not frigid, Anna. You're frustrated. That's why you suffer from so many headaches. You're sexually starved.'

I leapt to my feet. 'You're disgusting and insufferable!' I cried furiously. 'I'm going home – and what's more, I'm never coming back!'

Chapter Twenty-eight

I STAYED AWAY a week. Oliver made no comment when I came back. Nor did he apologize.

On the rare occasions he was home for the weekend, we went for long walks and sometimes he took me to an art gallery, never allowing me to see more than a dozen selected pictures. Occasionally he took me to a play. He made no attempt to kiss me again.

'Oliver,' I said one evening when we were sitting on the sofa sipping our coffee. 'Have you ever been in love?'

'In love!' he said cynically. 'For God's sake, must you always wrap everything in pink tissue paper. Why don't you ask me if I've been sexually attracted to a woman?'

'Because that's not what I mean.'

'It's the same thing, Anna. What's the difference? You were what you call in love with the clodhopper. Don't try and tell me you weren't sexually attracted to him.'

I could feel the colour rise to my cheeks. 'Stop always talking about Johan.'

'What's your definition of being in love?'

I thought how often I'd felt an impulse to brush Johan's soft hair from his forehead. I looked at Oliver's crisp fair hair. The thought of touching it frightened me.

'What are you thinking about?' he said, looking at me suspiciously. 'Why are you looking at my hair?'

I blushed guiltily.

'Ah.' He smiled sarcastically. 'You'd an inclination to run your fingers through the clodhopper's hair. I can read you like a book, my girl.'

'You haven't answered my question, Oliver. Have you ever been in love?'

'I've been sexually attracted, frequently.'

'Hasn't it ever meant more than that? Have you never felt tenderness or love for a woman?'

'There are times, Anna, when I find your sentimentality positively nauseating.'

'Don't you want to marry one day and have children?'

'God forbid!'

During the autumn Uncle Charles and Aunt Elizabeth drove me through the countryside and I marvelled at the rich autumnal colours – the opulent varying shades of red and russet and the bright clear yellows.

Suddenly winter was upon us and Christmas approached. I'd been so steeped in my unhappiness during the previous Christmas at The Oaks that it had passed almost unnoticed. Now I was bewitched by the white snowclad landscape. I helped Aunt Elizabeth decorate the tree and hang up the holly and mistletoe. We wrapped our presents and placed them under the tree.

Trina wrote: 'This year the Christmas lunch is at Wonderkloof. The second Christmas that you haven't been with us – it won't be the same without you, darling. We all miss you so much.

'I suppose Maria's told you she's expecting? The baby's due in January and Bettie has knitted enough woollies to clothe an entire crèche.

'Pieter is now as tall as Johannes and I regret to say, is already showing a lively interest in girls.'

Christmas cards and presents arrived from South Africa. I added the parcels to those stacked under the tree.

'Here's another card for you, dear,' Aunt Elizabeth said one morning a few days before Christmas, holding it out while she looked through the post.

I took the large rectangular envelope and saw that it was addressed in Johan's handwriting. My fingers clenched and I stared at it transfixed.

Aunt Elizabeth looked up. 'Aren't you going to open it?'

I did so slowly. It contained a mounted photograph of the old homestead, taken in the brilliant winter sunshine when it wasn't masked by the two oaks. I looked at it silently, feeling a lump in my throat. I must tear it up, I thought. With numb fingers I opened the card. 'When are you coming home?' he'd written in his characteristic firm handwriting. I didn't tear it up. I had the picture framed and put it on my dressing-table. The other half of the card I hid between the handkerchiefs in my drawer.

Now that it was winter, Oliver fetched me when he wanted me to spend the evening with him. He always telephoned first. 'I'll fetch you at eight o'clock,' he'd say abruptly. 'See that you're ready when I come: I don't want to chitterchatter to your Uncle and Aunt.'

This evening, when we entered his study, the fire was lit, the curtains drawn and the muted reds made the room warm and glowing.

I took off my coat and handed my present to him. 'Here's a little present for you, Oliver.'

'Thanks.' He took it without noticing the delicate Christmas wrapping or the silver ribbon and ruthlessly tore it open. 'Well, it's the first time a woman's given me a tie I'm prepared to wear,' he said graciously. He

207

nodded towards the bookcase. 'There's a present for you on top of the bookcase. Don't open it now – it's a book on impressionistic art.'

'Oh, Oliver. Please let me open it!'

'No, you may do so at home.' He sat down next to me.

'Aren't you working tonight?'

'No.' He put his arms around me. 'Now don't get all tensed up, Anna. This is just a little Christmas kiss.' Then he pushed me away irritably. 'God Almighty, you're an unsatisfactory woman to kiss!'

'You've no tenderness in you.' I looked at his hard chiselled face.

'Tenderness!' He leant back and stretched out his long slim legs. 'Must you always use these sentimental expressions. I suppose you think your clodhopper has tenderness?'

'If you must always talk about Johan, at least call him by his name.'

'I prefer to call him the clodhopper. D'you think he has tenderness?'

'I know he has. Both tenderness and compassion.'

He drew his legs up. 'He's probably a goddamned lousy lover.'

'I suppose you think you're a better one,' I said, stung into being childish.

He smiled complacently. 'I think I'm pretty good – at least, so I've been told.'

'I'm not the slightest bit interested in your love life,' I said distantly.

He leaned over and kissed me gently on the mouth. 'How's that for a little bit of tenderness?' I felt a faint tingling down my spine. He sensed it immediately and drew me into his arms and kissed me again. 'Aren't you interested, Anna?' He stroked my hair from my brow.

'Interested in what?'

'In sex, or love as you so romantically call it. Don't you want to know what it's all about – how old are you?'

'You know my age perfectly well.'

'Twenty-three and still a virgin!'

'Really, Oliver! You say that as though it's something indecent.'

'Hardly indecent, my girl – but certainly unique.'

He kissed me and leant over me, his mouth poised above mine – his eyes bright and clear as sapphires. 'Let me teach you about love,' he whispered.

'But I'm not in love with you!'

'Forget all that sentimental twaddle about being in love. It will be wonderful, Anna, I promise you – you'll enjoy it.'

'What a horrible cold-blooded idea!'

He put his mouth on mine and drew me to him until I felt as though I was drowning; then he took my face in his hands. 'It will be neither cold-blooded nor horrible,' he said softly.

'What about Uncle Charles and Aunt Elizabeth? What will they think about it?'

'My dear girl, don't be naïve. Surely you don't suppose we're going to tell them?' He nuzzled my ear. 'Let's go away for a weekend,' he whispered.

'Is that what happens when you disappear nearly every weekend?'

He stiffened. 'I've told you before. Mind your own business.'

I disengaged myself and sat up straight. 'I've no intention of having an affair with you, Oliver.'

He smiled and ran his cool hand up my arm. 'Don't just discard the idea,' he said quietly. 'Think about it.'

Chapter Twenty-nine

'MARIA'S BABY is a boy, as you doubtless know,' Trina wrote. 'He bears a remarkable resemblance to Gert, with his red face and slightly protuberant eyes. I only hope the poor child won't inherit his grandfather's ways. Maria tells me that she's asked you to be the baby's godmother. So you now have two god-children!

'As you know, Maria had the baby at Mooi Vlei. Bettie, needless to say, is in ecstasies and clucks over the child all day. Fond as I am of her, I must admit I'm finding her tiresome and will be glad when the baby's gone so that it will be possible to have an intelligible conversation with her again.

'We've had a wonderful crop and have been very busy.

'Johannes is at last himself; there are times when he's silent but the unhappiness and strain has left his face.

'Darling, I've had a wonderful idea. I'd decided to fly to England in May to see you. Now I've a yearning to see the Matterhorn once more before I die. Jan and I saw it seventeen years ago and vowed that we'd return. That was not to be. I want to see it with you. Do you remember how many times I've spoken to you about that wonderful mountain?

'On making enquiries I find your booking can be

arranged from here. I thought we'd meet at the Seilers Hotel in Zermatt on the first of May. All the bookings have been made and your ticket will be posted to you. I hope you'll like my idea. I'm longing to see you and can tell from your letters that you're happy and yourself again.'

There was a postscript. 'This Oliver you mention from time to time. Is he the rather conceited self-centred young architect living with his mother in the house next door?'

'I envy you,' Uncle Charles said. 'Elizabeth and I have always meant to go to Zermatt, but you know how time flies. Somehow we've never been able to get there.'

'Why don't you go in May and join us?'

'It's a kind thought, my dear, but I think Trina would like to have you to herself. When you write tell her that we hope she'll spend some time with us at The Oaks.'

Oliver didn't refer to his proposition for a couple of months. He kissed me on rare occasions, but when he did so, the kiss deepened.

At the beginning of April he disappeared on one of his mysterious weekends and came back bad-tempered and disgruntled.

He barely greeted me the following evening and when we entered the study, took off his coat and went straight to his desk. I read and then leant back, closed my eyes and listened to the music. I opened them when it suddenly stopped.

'Why did you turn that off? It's your favourite record.'

He was looking down at me with an annoyed expression. Without replying he sank down and pulled me into his arms. The kiss was long and passionate and at the end of it I was shaken and he was breathing unevenly.

211

'Well, have you thought about it?' His face was close to mine and his arms still around me.

'About what?'

'Don't be coy, Anna. You know what I'm talking about.' His mouth was next to my ear and I could hear his quick breathing.

'Yes, Oliver, I've thought about it and haven't changed my mind.'

He moved away and sat back, folding his arms, his face cold and hard. 'Well, I've changed mine.'

'What d'you mean?' I stared at him.

'I mean what I said. I'm no longer interested in this abortive unsatisfying love-making.' He smiled slightly. 'I've now a definite urge to make love to you – if you're not prepared to satisfy this urge, there's really no point in seeing each other anymore.'

'But why can't we—'

'As far as I'm concerned, it's to be all or nothing,' he interrupted.

'B-but that's blackmail, Oliver,' I stammered.

'Call it what you like. That's how I feel. I can't go on like this.'

'You mean you don't want me to come here again?'

He smiled rather tensely. 'Not unless you're prepared to play it my way.' I looked at him speechlessly. 'You don't have to make up your mind in a hurry, but I don't want to see you until you've done so. When you've decided one way or the other, let me know.' He stood up and put on his coat, then took my hands, pulled me to my feet, and kissed me gently. 'Come, I'll take you home.'

It took me two weeks to make up my mind. Two weeks in which I missed him more and more with each passing day. I missed his stimulating company, his caustic

212

tongue and his dry wit. I yearned to see his thin sardonic face and longed to feel his mouth on mine and experience the growing excitement of his kisses. At night the light in his window beckoned to me across the lawn. I prowled restlessly about the house, unable to occupy myself. Much as I loved Uncle Charles and Aunt Elizabeth, they were dull company in comparison to Oliver.

Aunt Elizabeth noticed that I was preoccupied and restless. 'Have you and Oliver had a quarrel, dear?'

'No,' I mumbled.

'He hasn't been over to fetch you for some time.' I muttered inaudibly. She crinkled her eyes. 'Why don't you run over after dinner and make it up.' If only you knew his evil intentions, I thought bitterly.

I stole across the lawn one night and stood where I could see into his window. He was leaning back staring moodily in front of him, the end of his pencil clenched between his teeth. I quickly turned away, fearful that he might see me.

When I ultimately went to him, I stood outside the door for several minutes before I found the courage to knock and open it.

He quickly looked up as the door opened, the light above him accentuating the hard planes of his face. 'Well?'

I hung my head and scuffed the Turkish carpet. 'All right, Oliver,' I mumbled. 'I'll do it.'

'Good,' he said crisply, as though I'd accepted an invitation to dinner. 'Sit down and listen to the music. I'll join you in a minute.'

I sat on the sofa trying to overcome my nervousness. When he sank down next to me, I had a moment of sheer panic and started to tremble. He took me in his arms and laid his cheek against mine. Then held me away and looked at me and kissed me gently. 'How's that for tenderness?' He smiled. 'Don't look so frightened, Anna. You could be a sacrificial lamb.'

'I feel rather like one.'

He laughed softly, kissed me and started to unbutton my dress.

I caught his hands. 'No, Oliver, not now!'

'What d'you mean?'

'I don't want you to make love to me until I've had my holiday with Trina.'

'What has she to do with us?'

'Please, Oliver! She'll know the minute she sees me that something's happened. You always say what a tell-tale face I have – Trina can read me as easily as you do.'

'For God's sake,' he said impatiently. 'You're nearly twenty-four. Surely you're not going to let that old dragon dictate to you.' He grinned sardonically. 'Don't you worry, she's had an affair or two.'

I drew away and looked at him angrily. 'If you call Trina a dragon again, or refer to Johan as a clodhopper, I'll go home and never come back. This time I mean it!'

He smiled disarmingly and drew me into his arms. 'Calm down,' he said softly.

'I'll go away with you the weekend after I get back,' my voice trembled.

His arms tightened. 'I know of a cottage in Scotland where we could stay,' he whispered.

'Have you been there on one of your weekends?'

His face froze. 'My God!' he said angrily. 'D'you think I'd take you where I've been with another woman? Are you crazy!'

'I thought—'

'I don't want to hear what you thought!' He moved irritably.

'Is the cottage near a stream?' I asked placatingly. 'Has it a thatched roof and roses growing up the walls?'

'What on earth are you talking about?'

I smiled. 'I was thinking of the picture above the mantelpiece in my room. It's such a romantic little cottage.'

'You and your romantic twaddle,' he grumbled, but he smiled and buried his lips in my hair – his face strangely luminous and soft.

'Oliver,' my voice shook. 'I may spoil everything – I mightn't be able to stop myself getting emotionally involved.'

He looked as though I'd hit him over the head with a sandbag. His face tightened and he crushed me against his body.

'Oliver! You're hurting me!'

He pushed me away and jumped to his feet. 'Go home!' he said unevenly. 'Go on, go home, you blasted little idiot, before we start having our affair tonight!'

Chapter Thirty

I OPENED THE door and stepped out of the train on to the platform of the small station at Zermatt. The sun was shining and the air was clean and sharp. A porter from the Seilers Hotel touched his cap and took my suitcase and I followed him to the hotel, which was a few minutes' walk from the station. I paused on the way to stare silently at the Matterhorn, shielding my eyes against the blinding glare of the snow. I gazed in awe at the soaring challenging spire – frightened and chilled by its forbidding splendour.

I was greeted at the desk with the news that Trina had gone for a walk and would meet me in the small room beyond the lounge at seven o'clock.

It was already late afternoon and I sat at my bedroom window, which faced the Matterhorn, and watched the snow on the towering peak become tinged with pink and fade to pearly grey. The terrifying slate-grey cliffs darkened to an ominous black.

At half past six I changed into a soft woollen dress. It was a subtle shade of almond green which was flattering to my eyes and skin. I combed my hair and carefully made up my eyes. When I finally appraised myself in the long mirror, I was satisfied that Trina would be suitably impressed.

At ten past seven I dashed across the foyer and practically ran through the lounge, quickly entering the room beyond.

'Trina!' I cried.

In two steps he reached me and kissed my cheek. 'Hallo, Anna, how are you?'

He was wearing his courting clothes and a silk tie I'd given him for Christmas two years ago.

I stared at him in disbelief, feeling myself go pale.

'What are you doing here?' I just managed to whisper.

He grinned. 'I've come to see the Matterhorn.'

'You've come to see the Matterhorn?' I repeated in a whisper.

He drew out a chair. 'Sit down, Anna.'

I almost collapsed into it and mutely watched him take the opened champagne bottle from the ice-bucket and fill his glass and mine. He placed the long-stemmed glass in front of me, then lifted his own and smiled. 'Welcome to Zermatt!'

I picked up mine with cold fingers and put it down untasted. Feeling his eyes on me I twisted the stem in my fingers.

'You're looking wonderful. You've put on weight – and I like the way you're doing your hair.'

'Where's Trina?'

'Ma? She's at Wonderkloof.'

'At Wonderkloof!' He was trying not to smile. 'You m-mean she's not coming?' I stuttered.

'No. She never intended coming. She thought I needed a holiday and suggested I should see the Matterhorn. I was aggreeable and she organized everything in her usual efficient manner.'

The blood rushed to my face. 'How did you know I would be here? Did Trina tell you?'

'No, she never said a word. I have, however, the

greatest confidence in her powers of organization: as soon as I arrived I checked to make certain you were coming.'

The blood throbbed in my temples. 'How dare she! How dare she do this to me!'

'Come, Anna. Where's your sense of humour?'

I looked at his smiling face with hatred. 'Sense of humour!' I cried angrily. 'I fail to find anything faintly humorous in this situation.' I looked at him, the hot blood burning my cheeks. 'Say it, Johan! Go on, say it – Ma and her matchmaking!'

He burst out laughing. I clenched my hand in fury and he quickly grasped it with his warm fingers. 'Anna—'

I snatched it away. 'Well, Johan,' I said, having difficulty in controlling my breathing. 'This is the one time you don't have to worry about the girl Trina's foisted on you. I'm going to bed and will leave Zermatt tomorrow.'

'Ma hasn't foisted you on me, I wanted to see you.' I picked up my bag. 'Wait, Anna. Give me a chance to talk to you.'

'What can we possibly have to say to each other?'

'Don't be ridiculous. We've never had difficulty talking in the past. Why should we have nothing to say now?'

I could feel the first signs of a headache. 'I'm going to bed. I'll never forgive Trina for this. Never as long as I live!'

'Anna,' he said quietly. 'Don't be so damned obstinate. Listen to what I've to say.'

'I won't listen and I never want to see you again!' I jumped up and ran blindly out of the room.

I locked my door and took two tablets with a shaking hand, then lay on my bed trying to quell the feverish turmoil in my mind. 'I hate Trina!' I whispered. 'And I hate Johan!'

218

My body was tense and trembling and it felt as though a nail was being driven into the base of my skull. I lay still, trying to discipline my body and mind. The headache slowly subsided and as the tablets took effect, I became drowsy and fell into an uneasy sleep.

I awoke with a start to hear someone knocking on my door.

'Who's there?'

'It's me, Johan. Open the door. I want to speak to you.'

'Go away!' I shouted angrily.

'Open the door, Anna.'

'No, I won't!'

'If you don't open this damned door, I'll break it down!'

I remained silent.

A loud crash made me sit up in alarm. 'Stop it, Johan!'

There was a second crash louder and more deafening than the first.

'Oh, how can you behave like this!' I cried. I ran across the room and unlocked the door. 'You should be ashamed of yourself!' I looked apprehensively up and down the passage.

He was dishevelled and hot. He grinned, straightened his tie and brushed his hair back. 'As Ma'd say, you're pig-headed.'

'She says that about you, not me.'

We smiled.

'You'll stay, won't you?' His voice was warm and he took my hand.

'It seems so pointless,' I muttered.

'Stay, Anna, if only for tomorrow. We'll spend the day in the open and have dinner together. I promise if you still want to leave the next day, I won't lift a finger to stop you. Will you?'

'Yes,' I muttered without looking at him.

'That's fine. I'll order a picnic lunch tomorrow morning.'

I said nothing and withdrew my hand.

'Well, I'll be off to bed. I'm glad your headache's better. Good-night, and sleep well.' He kissed my cheek.

He was very close to me. I put my hands against his chest and pushed him with all my strength; for a second I caught sight of his outraged face as he reeled backwards across the corridor.

'I'm sick and tired of your goddamned brotherly kisses!' I shouted.

I slammed the door, locked it and burst into tears. I threw myself on the bed and wept unrestrainedly. Not tears of sorrow, but tears of rage and shame. That wicked interfering old woman! I'd never forgive her. Never to my dying day! She'd used me like a pawn and in so doing had re-opened a wound and robbed me of my hard-earned peace of mind.

I knew now that I still loved Johan – that I'd always loved him. I shuddered – I'd practically told him so! Oh, how could I have shouted that at him, and worst of all, using Oliver's blasphemous language. As for having an affair with Oliver – the very thought of it made me feel ill. I never wanted to see either of them again.

Early the next morning I put on my travelling suit, packed my bag and went down to the desk at half past seven. I was early, but not early enough.

Johan was standing in the foyer and greeted me with a wide smile. 'Good-morning.'

'Good-morning,' I muttered, my colour rising.

I rang the bell and fidgeted. 'Where's the manager?'

'He's gone to see about our picnic lunch.'

'I'm not going with you, Johan. I'm leaving this morning.'

'Why?'

'Because I've changed my mind.'

'What are you running away from?' He looked at me steadily.

'I'm not running away from anything,' I said loudly.

He smiled. 'Please stay, Anna. Just for today. Even if it's only to please me.' He'd never pleaded with me before. He took my arm. 'Come, I'll walk with you to your room and wait in the corridor while you change.' I meekly allowed him to lead me to the lift.

We walked up the narrow cobbled streets of Zermatt which had never seen traffic. We paused at the little Church and the grave-yard where the mountaineers who perished on the Matterhorn lie buried.

'I don't mind telling you, that damned mountain scares me. It's too cold and formidable for my taste.' He looked up at the slender peak. 'But I admit I can appreciate its challenge.'

We wandered through the macabre museum near the churchyard, looking at the photographs of the climbers who had plunged to their death – some to lie forever buried in the deep snow at the foot of the dark cliffs. Johan paused for a long time in front of the photograph of a beautiful German girl. We saw the poignant relics they'd left behind – a piece of frayed rope, a boot, an icepick.

I shivered.

'Come,' he took my arm. 'Let's get out of this place.'

We walked in silence, following the footpath and later picnicked on a green verge amongst great rocks. I was at peace and happy – glad I'd stayed because this was a day I would remember all my life.

He sat leaning against a rock, clear-eyed, and relaxed.

'You're looking well, Johan.'

'So are you.' He grinned. 'Where have you learned such lurid language?' I blushed and looked down to hide my embarrassment. 'I enjoyed the letters you wrote Ma.'

'Oh.' I looked up. 'I didn't know you read them.'

'Yes, I read them with great interest.' He picked a blade of grass and put it between his teeth. 'I met Oliver Bates once.'

I felt myself turn a fiery red. 'You've met Oliver?' I said self-consciously.

He threw the blade of grass away and looked at me closely. 'Yes. I played rugby against him when the Springboks toured the British Isles.'

'You played rugby against Oliver!' I cried. 'I can't believe it! He never mentioned that he'd ever played. In fact he's rather disparaging about people who do.'

'He played centre for Cambridge. In that particular match he scored a brilliant try. Many people think he would have been capped for England if he hadn't given it up the following year – are you in love with him?'

If he'd asked me this yesterday I would have said, 'I don't know – I honestly don't know.' Now I looked away and said quietly, 'No, I don't love him.'

He moved over to me and stretched himself on the grass, laying his head on my lap. 'The alpine air's made me sleepy.'

He looked up and took my hand, but I quietly took it away and leant back against the rock and closed my eyes. Later when I felt his breathing become regular, I looked down on his sleeping face and felt an overwhelming impulse to brush the soft hair off his forehead.

Chapter Thirty-one

THE PALE HONEY-COLOURED dress I wore had once caused Oliver to raise an eyebrow and comment dryly, 'Your taste in clothes has improved.'

I met Johan in the hotel lounge at eight o'clock. He stood up as I came in and looked me over appreciatively. 'I like your dress.'

'And you're wearing your courting cl—' I stopped aghast and my cheeks flamed when I saw him grin.

The nightclub where we dined was dimly lit and intimate. A lantern glowed in the centre of each table making a small pool of light – ours made dark caverns of his eyes and accentuated his chin.

As the evening progressed I tried to memorize and cherish each moment as I'd done throughout the day. I studied his face as though I'd never seen it before, trying to fix it indelibly in my mind. This is probably the last time I'll see him, I thought. But I'm happy. I'm happier at this moment than I've ever been.

'What are you thinking about, Anna?'

I smiled dreamily. 'Nothing in particular.'

'Shall we dance?'

I picked up my glass, and quickly drained it. 'Let's dance later. I'd love a little more champagne.'

He filled my glass. I twisted the stem and smiled at him. 'How long d'you intend staying here, Johan?'

'It depends. I haven't made up my mind. What about you?'

'I'll return to London tomorrow.'

The music started again. The passionate throbbing song made me catch my breath and move uneasily. I turned my head and saw a man clasp his partner more closely to his body.

'Let's dance.'

'No!' I cried involuntarily. I was panic stricken and my heart was beating too fast. I took a quick sip of champagne. 'I'm enjoying this so much. Can't we dance later?'

Instead of returning my smile; he took the glass from my fingers and put it on the other side of the table. 'You've had enough champagne, and we're going to dance now.' He pushed his chair back, stood and looked down at me. When I remained seated his chin became prominent. 'Get on your feet, Anna.'

I got up slowly and followed him on to the floor. I held myself rigidly in his arms trying to divorce myself from the music which quickened my blood. As soon as it stopped I turned to go back to our table, but he caught my arm and held me. 'Don't be in such a damned hurry. The dance isn't over yet.'

The same haunting tune started and he drew me suddenly into his arms and pressed his mouth against my cheek. 'Relax, darling,' he whispered.

Darling. That warm and lovely word so often lightly used. My eyes filled with tears and my body melted. He gathered me closer and laid his cheek against mine and we danced in silence.

When the music stopped he looked down and gently touched my face. 'Your cheeks are wet, darling.'

224

'Stop calling me darling,' I sobbed. I slipped from his arms and quickly crossed to our table and opened my bag, taking out an inadequate wisp of lace, I dried my eyes. He pulled his chair closer to mine until we were sitting shoulder to shoulder and took my hand looking at it absently, then he turned it over and buried his warm mouth in the centre of my palm. Instinctively my fingers curved and cupped his face and the tears trickled down my cheeks. He passed me his handkerchief and keeping my head down, I dried my eyes and blew my nose. 'It's no use,' I said choking. 'I don't know what's wrong with me.' I shook my head. 'I can't stop crying. Will you take me back to the hotel.' He nodded and signalled to the waiter.

We walked down the narrow cobbled street and he linked his arm with mine, taking my hand and lacing our fingers. 'This is how the students at Stellenbosch University walk with their girl-friends.' He matched his step with mine.

We entered the hotel and I averted my face so that the night porter wouldn't see my tear-stained eyes. We stood with fingers interlaced in the lift and it was only when we stopped outside my door that he relinquished my hand so that I could open my bag and fumble for the key. He took it from me, unlocked the door and pushed it open, handing the key back to me.

I looked at him, trying to smile. 'Good-night, Johan. I'm sorry, I've ruined your whole evening.'

There was a hint of a smile in his grey eyes. 'The evening has only begun,' he said, and bundled me unceremoniously into my room, closing the door behind us. He reached for me in the dark and drew me swiftly into his arms. 'No brotherly kisses tonight, my darling,' he whispered – and I could tell that he was smiling.

He stretched across, switched on the bedside lamp and leant over me, looking at me rather seriously.

I felt shy and lifted my hand, shielding my face from the bright light. 'Why've you switched on the light, Johan? I look like hell.'

He smiled. 'You do,' he agreed. He touched my eyelids. 'Puffy eyes.' He tweaked the tip of my nose. 'A red nose.' He kissed me very gently. 'And a lovely mouth.' Then he put his arm around me. 'I've switched on the light because I want to talk about Sarah.' My body stiffened and he held me closer. 'We must talk about her, darling, otherwise she'll always be between us. We'll talk about her now, and then if you wish it, we'll never mention her again.'

His face was very close to mine and I reached up, brushing his hair off his forehead. It was thicker and springier than I'd expected.

'By the time I'd been married to Sarah for six weeks, I knew that I'd made the biggest mistake of my life.' He was no longer looking at me – I was forgotten and he was back in the past. 'At first I thought she was jealous and possessive, but I soon realized it was something far beyond that. By the time we went to Johannesburg, shortly after you and Ma got back, I was convinced that she wasn't normal. She was untruthful and there was a lack of balance and a dangerous streak in her which frightened me. I went to see her brother: to begin with he was cagey and I was unable to get anything out of him. I was pretty overwrought at the time: when he wouldn't speak I grabbed him by the shirt front and shook him – and he broke down completely. He told me that their mother committed suicide when Sarah was four, and there's a maiden aunt in a mental institution. Sarah showed her first signs of abnormality when she was seventeen. She was devoted to her father and

226

became obsessively jealous of her stepmother.' He lifted himself and put his weight on his elbow and looked down at me, his face very close to mine. 'There was a pekinese.'

I stiffened. 'A pekinese?'

'Yes. It belonged to her stepmother – Sarah killed it.'

I cried out and covered my face.

'Don't, darling.' He took my hands from my face and kissed me. 'I love you – that's the only thing that matters. We love each other and we're together now.'

'How did she kill it?' I whispered.

He hesitated. 'She threw it out of the upstairs window.'

My eyes filled with tears. 'Is that what she—'

He put his hand over my mouth. 'Hush, darling, listen to the rest of the story.' He held me until he felt me relax. 'She started a campaign against her stepmother and succeeded in wrecking the marriage and driving her from the house. After about six months, her father and stepmother started seeing each other again. He was very much in love with her and wanted her to come back to him but she refused to do so while Sarah was still there. One night he called Sarah into his study and told her that his wife was returning to him and that he had arranged for her to stay with her aunt. Four hours later, when her brother came into the study, he found Sarah sitting in a chair and his father lying dead on the floor.'

I stared at him. 'Did she kill him?'

'No, he died of a heart attack – two, to be exact. She sat with him for three and a half hours during which time he had two heart attacks – the second killed him. She made no attempt to 'phone a doctor, nor did she lift a finger to help him. She just sat and watched him.' He put his weight on his elbow again, his face taut and strained. 'Anna, things happened between Sarah and

227

me which I'll never tell you. I married her and owe her loyalty.' He looked so unhappy that I placed my finger on his mouth and he pressed it to his lips. 'I was half in love with you when I met her, though I didn't know it. I was completely bowled over by her beauty. Only after ⊤ was married to her and realized my mistake, did I know how deeply I loved you.' He took my face in his hands. 'I'd see you every day and know that I'd lost you.' A shadow came over his face. 'That's something I have to live with. Did Sarah know? Did she sense what I felt for you – was that why she turned against you?' He looked at me gravely. 'I knew that she'd turned against you and could see history repeating itself. There was nothing I could do to help you. That's why I told you to leave Wonderkloof.'

'Oh, you hurt me so much! You'll never know how much.'

'I knew, darling. You looked as though I'd mortally wounded you.'

'Johan, what made you return from Johannesburg a day early?'

'It was very odd. At twelve o'clock I was walking down Eloff Street when I stopped dead in my tracks with the awful conviction that something had happened to you.'

'That's about the time she pushed me over the edge. I screamed for you as I fell.' He buried his face in my neck and put his arms under my waist, tightening them until our bodies were interlocked. 'Johan, what happened to Chiang?' He drew me closer and kissed the hollow in my throat. 'Tell me what happened to him!'

'*Ou* Attie found him underneath your window.' His voice was muffled. 'I buried him before you and Ma came home.'

'Was he d-dead when you found him?' I stammered, my body rigid.

He leaned over and switched off the light. I gasped as

his arms closed around me and his mouth found mine. Then Chiang and all else was forgotten.

He sat on the edge of my bed and pulled on his socks, looking happy and relaxed. He looked at me and grinned. 'I'll have to make an honest woman of you.'

'You don't have to. In fact, I'd rather enjoy being your mistress.'

I expected him to smile, but he looked at me rather sternly. 'We'll get married at once. Today if possible.'

'You haven't asked me if I want to marry you,' I grumbled.

He smiled. 'Will you?'

I nodded mutely, then cleared my throat. 'There's a condition attached, Johan.'

'Why don't you call me darling?'

I suddenly felt shy. 'I'm not mentally adjusted to what's happened. I still can't believe it. I couldn't possibly call you that yet. Can you understand?' I asked timidly.

He took my hand and kissed it. 'Yes, I think I can – but don't wait too long. Well, what's your condition?'

'You mustn't tell Trina we're married. I must spend two weeks with Uncle Charles and Aunt Elizabeth before I leave. I can't pack my bags and go.'

'Why not?'

'No, I can't! I owe them my sanity and happiness. I must leave them graciously.

'They'd understand if you went with me.'

'I know they would, but I know how much they'd appreciate it if I spent a little time with them before I go.'

'Well, if you feel so strongly about it, I won't stop you.'

'And d'you promise not to tell Trina?'

'I don't think you realize what Ma's been through the last two years. She'd be very happy if she knew we're now married.'

Johan had suffered and so had I. But not Trina! She'd doubted me and in the end had used me like a pawn.

'D'you promise, Johan?'

'Yes,' he said reluctantly. 'I promise.'

He had put on his clothes and walked over to the dressing-table, picked up my comb and ran it through his hair, then came and sat on the edge of my bed.

'Anna, why did you blush so violently when I mentioned Oliver Bates?' I immediately blushed again. He looked at me suspiciously. 'I was pretty certain that you loved me when you swore at me and pushed me across the passage.'

'I didn't swear at you!'

'You went as red as a beetroot when I mentioned his name. I thought maybe you'd had an affair with him – I now know that wasn't so.' I knew I was the picture of guilt. 'Why did you blush – and what are you looking so damned guilty about now?' He was regarding me far too closely for my comfort. 'Answer me!'

'I was about to have an affair with him,' I muttered.

'You were what! But you told me you weren't in love with the fellow!' I avoided his eyes. 'When was this affair to take place?'

I felt cornered. I slipped further under the bedcovers, trying to make myself small. 'Oh, Johan, don't let's talk about it any more.'

His face was dark. 'We'll certainly talk about it. When was it to take place, Anna?'

'Next weekend,' I mumbled.

'Next weekend, my God!' There was a heavy silence and I didn't dare look at him. 'What in God's name were you thinking of! Had he asked you to marry him?'

'Marry him! Oliver doesn't believe in love and marriage. He thought I ought to know something about sex.' I glanced at him and was frightened by the expression on his face. 'He said it would improve me,' I faltered.

'I'd like to knock his damned block off! As for you,' he said slowly, 'I ought to spank your little bottom!'

I clutched the bedclothes and drew them to my chin. 'Please, don't be so cross with me – I can't bear it!' He took off his jacket and started to unknot his tie. 'Johan, why are you taking off your clothes!'

He took off his shoes and looked at me angrily. 'You know why.'

Chapter Thirty-two

WE HAD TO wait ten days before we could get married. I wrote and broke the news to Uncle Charles and Aunt Elizabeth, begging them to keep the secret from Trina. We spent a further week in Switzerland and three days in Paris. Then Johan came back with me to The Oaks, spending two days there before returning to South Africa.

'Of all improbable things,' I whispered in the middle of the night. 'I never dreamt that I'd ever share this bed with you.'

'Uh-huh,' he grunted disinterestedly, already half asleep.

When I awoke the next morning he was standing at my dressing-table holding the photograph of the old homestead. He looked up and saw that I was awake. 'You've had this framed.'

'Yes.'

He looked at it again and I knew that Wonderkloof was calling him back – I could feel he was becoming restive.

At London Airport he drew me aside. 'Anna, as soon as you return you're to tell Ma we're married. You're not to keep her on a string. She's taken enough punishment on our behalf and I feel guilty that she's not sharing in our happiness.'

'I promise I'll tell her.'

'And keep away from that bounder next door. I'm not altogether happy about leaving you here.'

'Really, Johan! I wish I'd never told you about Oliver – you're always harping on about him.'

'I don't trust him!'

'He wouldn't even look at me now.'

'He'd better not,' he looked at me sternly. Then he smiled and kissed me. 'Goodbye, darling. I'll miss you like hell.' He shook hands with Uncle Charles, kissed Aunt Elizabeth and quickly walked away without looking back. I watched him until he disappeared through the doorway.

I missed him so much that there were times when I regretted that I had stayed behind. Uncle Charles knew how I felt and put his arm around me. 'It was good of you to stay, Anna – Elizabeth and I appreciate your unselfishness. You know how much we'll miss you, my child – we've come to think of you as our daughter.'

'You and Aunt Elizabeth will come to Wonderkloof for Christmas, won't you?'

'It was kind of Johan to suggest it.' He kept his arm around my shoulders. 'We'll be there for Christmas and are looking forward to it.'

Oliver telephoned the day before I left. 'Why haven't you been over to make me a cup of coffee?'

'I didn't know if you'd want to see me.'

'For God's sake, why not?' he said impatiently. 'Come around this evening.' I hesitated. He laughed shortly. 'Don't worry, my dear girl, I've no intention of making a pass at you.'

'All right. I'll come over at the usual time.'

'Good.' He slammed down the 'phone.

He was standing at the window when I came in and

slowly looked me up and down. 'The radiant bride!' he said sarcastically.

The colour rose to my cheeks. 'I don't know about being a radiant bride,' I said shyly, 'but I'm certainly a very happy one.'

He looked at me as though he found me more nauseating than usual. He waited for me to be seated, then sat down next to me. 'Did you know the clodhopper was going to be in Zermatt?'

'Of course not!'

'It must have been quite an agreeable surprise,' he said, with an offensive smile.

I shifted uncomfortably and tried to change the subject. 'Oliver, I was absolutely amazed when Johan told me that you'd played rugby for Cambridge.'

He looked at me coldly, his face expressionless. 'What's so amazing about it? It's not an achievement of which I'm particularly proud.' His lips tightened. 'So you and the clodhopper discussed me.'

'Don't be ridiculous, Oliver. Of course we didn't discuss you, and please stop calling Johan the clodhopper.'

'He's the clodhopper as far as I'm concerned.'

My temper flared. 'He's not a clodhopper!' I cried angrily. 'Nor's he a lousy lover,' I added childishly.

'For God's sake!' he said violently. 'Spare me the details of your love life.' He sat back and looked me over slowly and speculatively. 'You must have dropped into his hand like a goddamned ripe peach.'

'What d'you mean?'

'I mean what I say. You were so hot to have an affair, your blasted little tongue was hanging out!'

'Stop it, Oliver!' I cried angrily.

'I could have taken you any time I wanted.' He thrust his face into mine. 'And d'you know why I didn't?

234

Because I pandered to that plebeian, sentimental, romantic little mind of yours! I even found a thatched-roofed cottage next to a stream with roses growing over it. It was going to be love in a cottage all wrapped up in cellophane.'

'But there wasn't going to be any love.'

My remark seemed to goad him beyond endurance. His hard face turned dead white and he leapt up, dragging me roughly to my feet. 'Get out!' he said in a low concentrated voice. He pushed me across the room and opened the door. 'Go on, get out! Go back to your clodhopper – and don't come back, I don't want to see you again.' He thrust me out of the room and slammed the door.

I stood undecided in the passage and then timidly opened the door. He was standing at the window with his back to me.

'Goodbye, Oliver. I'm leaving tomorrow.'

'Goodbye, Anna,' he said quietly, without turning around.

I arrived at the airport in Cape Town on a bright clear winter's day. Walking across the tarmac I saw Trina, small and erect, waiting for me at the entrance. I felt such a warm flow of love that I ran the last few steps and clasped her in my arms. 'Oh, Trina, I'm so pleased to see you!'

She hugged and kissed me, then held me away looking me over, her brown eyes very bright. 'You look wonderful, darling. You're positively radiant!'

I hugged her again. 'That's because I'm so happy to see you.' We walked arm in arm to the car.

'You drive, darling. I want to sit back and look at you.' Later she patted my arm. 'Anna, I can't tell you how pleased I was when you wrote to say you were coming to stay: nor can you know what it means to me to see you so happy and well. I've never been able to forget what you looked like the last time I saw you – so thin, pale and unhappy – it's haunted me ever since. How long will you be staying with us, darling?'

'I've made no definite plans, I'll let you know when I've decided.'

She opened her bag and took out her cigarette case. 'Were you very angry with me?'

I felt again the rage and humiliation I'd suffered in Zermatt. 'How could you place me in such a painful position,' I said angrily. 'You knew that I was once in love with Johan – I'd told you so in my delirium. How could you throw us together like that! Surely you must have known how embarrassing it would be for me.' I glanced at her. 'There was a time I thought I'd never forgive you!'

She smiled and blew the smoke through her nostrils. 'But you've forgiven me now, haven't you, darling? And you were pleased to see Johannes, weren't you? I thought it would be such a lovely surprise for both of you.' I kept my eye on the road and made no reply. 'Johannes is looking so much better since his holiday. He's quite different – he looks happy and relaxed.' She paused and I felt her studying me. 'Did you see much of each other in Zermatt? Johannes, as usual, tells me nothing, though he did mention you were looking very well.'

'No, we didn't see much of each other. Johan was rather involved with a pretty little German girl.'

'He didn't mention that,' she said sharply.

'That's not altogether surprising,' I smiled.

She was silent for several minutes.

'The boys are looking forward so much to seeing you. Pieter will be here next weekend and you'll be amazed

236

to see how tall he is.' She stubbed out her cigarette. 'You must go for a walk with Johannes tomorrow morning and let him show you how much has been done on the farm while you've been away.'

I knew exactly how her mind was working. They'll go for walks. They'll see each other every day – perhaps they'll fall in love.

We swept around the bend and I saw the gracious square homestead gleaming white in the bright winter sun – as I'd seen it every morning on my dressing-table at The Oaks. This is my home now, I thought.

Trina could sense I was moved. 'Are you pleased to see the old house, darling?' My throat closed and I nodded, unable to answer her.

Bella heard the car and came to the front door to meet us. 'Welcome back, Miss Anna.' She looked at me, moist-eyed, and her pendulous lips unfolded in a tremulous smile. 'Miss Anna look well.' She knew I was in love.

Trina and I walked arm in arm through the garden. The deciduous trees had lost their leaves but the fat furry flower buds were forming on the magnolia tree. The bank of azaleas underneath the old pear tree made a brilliant splash of colour and the camellias bore bright heavy flowers amongst their shiny leaves.

Ou Christiaan was sweeping up the leaves. When he saw me his wrinkled face wreathed in a toothless grin. '*Klein Nooi* back! Now *Ou Nooi* heppy.'

Ou Attie looked up and nodded, giving a suspicion of a smile.

I heard Wolf bark. He was standing at the study door, staring at us, his ears sharply pricked.

'Wolf!' I cried.

He stood petrified, then dashed across the lawn and stopped in front of me. I knelt and he pushed into my arms, whining and licking my cheek. I fondled his head and held him close.

Trina's eyes were shining. 'How pleased we all are to see you, darling!'

He followed us into the sitting-room. The fire was lit and the room was scented by a bowl of violets on the sofa table. The tea table was placed next to Trina's chair and Johan was leaning against the mantelpiece.

'Hallo, Johan,' I said, not daring to look at him.

'Hallo, Anna.'

I saw Trina dart a quick look at us. Not even a brotherly kiss!

She pulled off her toque and tossed it on to the sofa and I stared at her speechlessly.

She looked at me and smiled, running her hand through her hair. 'You're looking at my hair. I've become as grey as an old badger.' She turned to Johan. 'I was telling Anna about the improvements on the farm. You must take her for a walk after breakfast to-morrow and show her what you've done.'

'Yes, Ma.'

'Actually,' I drawled, 'I've become rather lazy. I'm not so keen on going for walks after breakfast.'

When she remained silent I looked at her from beneath my lashes. I caught her off guard. Her shoulders were slumped and the lines of her face had sagged. She was a tired, grey-haired woman. Old, weary and defeated.

I caught my breath. For the first time I realized what she'd suffered and endured. I thought how she'd ceaselessly striven for my happiness and welfare and that of her two sons – never sparing herself. Meeting each crisis with indomitable courage. Looking at her, I was filled with shame and a deep love. The last drop of bitterness flowed from me.

238

I quickly turned to Johan. 'Darling!' I cried urgently.

In one bound he was across the room and caught me in his arms. He looked down and smiled. 'You called me darling.' Then he slowly and deliberately put his mouth on mine and with equal deliberation drew my body closer and closer until we were locked in a kiss of deepest passion. When he released me we were both breathing quickly and his narrowed eyes were glittering. 'Let's go to bed.'

'Really, Johan! We can't go to bed. It's only four o'clock!'

'What the hell does the time matter?'

I kept my arms around his neck and smiled. 'Shall we?' Then I gasped and clutched his arms. 'Trina!' I whispered fiercely.

His eyes widened in consternation. 'Good Lord, Ma!'

We turned to face her. He kept his arm around my waist and held me close to his side.

'We're married, Ma.'

She stood erect, shoulders squared and chin raised. Her mouth was quivering and the tears were streaming down her cheeks. Trina the indomitable, was crying.